Two's c# Three's a Coven

The Cosheston Chronicles

Jonathan Rowlands

Two's company, three's a Coven
Published by Jonathan Rowlands at Amazon Kindle
Copyright 2012 Jonathan Rowlands

Chapter One

"I don't like it down here; this place *really* gives me the creeps"!

"How so"?

"You only have to take a look around; everything about this place has *haunted* written all over it; it is dark……..it is also quite damp……..and even the *trees* look like trees possessed"! Mathew was honest and he was not at all afraid of being ridiculed. Mathew and his friend James were both thirteen year old lads of the parish and as usual they were up to little good.

"I am not altogether sure whether trees *can* become possessed"!

"There was a possessed tree in *Poltergeist* all right; the young Robbie Freleng almost got eaten alive by it in his back garden. And look at that gnarly and twisted looking thing over there"! and Mathew pointed. "It is fat and ugly and it has seemingly huge wooden boobies that are migrating down toward its waist"!

"Well……..such a thing is all too common with the advancing years; I have seen a few prime examples of the migrating boobies wandering around in this very village"! James was equally as sure. "But at the end of the day trees are just trees……nothing more; and you are probably just feeling a bit ill at ease because of all the things that your mother has told you about these woods"!

"Mothers usually have a knack of being right about such things"!

"Look; all the mums in this village tell their sons that Mill Bay Woods is a dark and brooding place teeming with dirty old men who have an unhealthy interest in young boys because the mums all know that of all the places in Cosheston *this* is the place most likely for their offspring to venture when embarking on their first experimental smoke; the story is probably told quite differently if the offspring involved are girls……..just so long as the end results are the same"! and James finished making their first experimental rollie with the few strands of tobacco that he had liberated from his dad's tobacco tin.

"I didn't know that you had to physically *make* cigarettes; I thought that you just bought them in packs of twenty and the like"!

"Nah; that's *way* too expensive these days; and *because* they are so expensive grown-ups tend to monitor their supply of ready-made cigarettes very closely; but who would possibly notice a little bit of tobacco going missing from a tin *full* of the stuff"!

"Just get a load of that almost *certainly* possessed tree a little way over there"! Mathew pointed and he started off on the haunted tree theme once again. "That one looks as though it has arms and legs and is happily ripping a baby limb from limb"!

"All I can see is a tree"! James rather uncommonly lied for he too could see the baby dismemberment that was going on if he squinted really hard. "I do hope that you remembered to bring some matches"!

Mathew stood up and he dug the box of matches out of his jeans pocket and he looked all around as he now assessed the trees that were closest to them.

"And just take a look at this huge tree that is just behind us; it looks like…………." but Mathew never finished his sentence. The lad just stood there and he stared; his mouth hanging open and his arm dropping back to his side as the colour drained from his cheeks.

"And what does *this* one look like to you, Captain Imagination; alien invaders from space, no doubt…….you haven't yet covered alien invaders from space"! and James turned to look at just what it was that Mathew was so consumed with.

The tree behind them was an Ash; not yet ravaged by the killer Ash dieback disease and probably of a good age given its enormous stature; and in the upper branches of the old Ash tree was a man; hanging by his neck from a thick rope; and the hanging man was all blue and bloated and hideous.

"Shit a brick"! James almost whispered.

"Shit a sodding *bungalow*; I think that I *will* take a drag of that rollie right about now"! Mathew replied in the same half whisper; but his best friend James had already dropped the handmade cigarette and he was running from the woods as fast as his legs would carry him.

"Wait for me; and give me those bloody matches back.......I have to put the matches back into stock otherwise I will surely be rumbled; and if *I* am rumbled then I promise that I will take *you* with me"! and Mathew was soon doing a very good job of catching up with his friend.

-2-

"What the bloody hell have we been called down to these God-forsaken woods for anyway"? wondered Detective Inspector Nigel Gallant.

"At least it isn't raining"! Detective Constable Theo Wiseman pointed out in his usual blue-skies way of thinking.

"I suppose that we have *that* much to be grateful for; but that over there is clearly a bloke hanging by his neck; and we investigate the *murders* and not the bloody suicides; especially on a Saturday afternoon during Six Nations season when Wales are playing Ireland and the pubs are open all bloody day"!

"Three"! said DC Wiseman.

"And will you stop with the counting of my bloody swearing"!

"Four"!

"He was dead a *long* time before he got anywhere near that tree"! said the *very* shapely lady pathologist. "Preliminary examination would suggest drowning to be the cause of death; but I would like to get him back and onto the slab before you quote me on anything"!

"Aha…………then I shall give you a ring at about four-thirty or thereabouts"! DI Gallant suggested to the very shapely lady pathologist. "And if you find any ID on the body then maybe I could pick that up later as well"?

"Four thirty………..that would be after the match then"!

"Look Jane……..it *is* Jane, isn't it; you yourself have to cut him open; the scenes of crime lot seem to be doing an excellent job of things over there and there doesn't seem much point in *everybody's* day being ruined; and I could always text you the scores as they happen……….virtually live"!

"There are witnesses to be interviewed; they are over there being comforted by the WPC's"!

"Comforted"?

"Comforted………..until their mums turn up; it was two young lads from the village that made the gruesome discovery"! and the very shapely lady pathologist pointed the boys out. "It's just that everything is taking so long because nobody can get a mobile phone signal down here; messages are having to be relayed and everything"!

"Aha………..two lads down here for an experimental smoke then, is it"?

"So it would seem".

"Right then Wiseman; you and I shall interview these boys as we are driving them home"! and DI Gallant suddenly seemed to cheer up the fair bit.

"Sir……..isn't the fair haired of the two boys the son from your local pub up in the village"? DC Wiseman seemed convinced.

"Is he…………I hadn't noticed"!

"Hang about for a minute; I don't recall seeing *that* on our way through the village"! DI Gallant was quite sure.

"You don't recall seeing *what*"? DC Wiseman wondered; but he carried on interviewing James and Mathew from the front passenger seat.

"That little car over there; it seems to have run down the hill from the estate and has crashed into the wall"! the Inspector explained and DC Wiseman turned around in his seat so that he might see for himself what had caught the attention of the Inspector.

"It must have been a low speed impact because of the lack of any real damage either to the car *or* the wall"! the Inspector was surmising. "But that much being said there is still some steam issuing from beneath the bonnet"! and DI Gallant brought their unmarked Police car to a halt just a few feet away from the runaway Peugeot. "We should have a quick look around just in case this runaway car has mowed anybody down in the estate; then we can get uniform onto it"!

"Gross"! Mathew told the Inspector.

"Could I come and have a look as well"? James wondered very politely.

"It wasn't so very long ago that you were running around in the woods and screaming for your mother"! the Inspector reminded the boy.

"It was just the shock of it all; I assure you that I am over that now"!

"Stay here………..*both of you*"! and the Detectives got out of their car and they inspected the lightly damaged Peugeot.

"Luckily enough there is nobody trapped underneath"! DC Wiseman was happy to report; and then he glanced along the street that led into the small estate just in case any victims had been left battered and bruised and lying in the road.

"Wiseman…………I don't suppose you happen to know how many scenes of crimes units we have in this force before we have to start drafting them in from neighbouring forces, do you"? the Inspector wondered of his junior colleague.

"Not offhand Sir; but bearing in mind the relatively small number of murders in these parts then I would hazard a guess at there being not that many"! and DC Wiseman was having a good old scratch at his head as he was speaking. "Why do you ask, Sir"?

"Because we are going to be needing another one"! and the Inspector invited DC Wiseman to have a little shifty in through the driver's door.

In the driver's seat was another corpse; quite obviously female this time; and just as blue and bloated and hideous as the body that had been discovered hanging from the Ash tree in the middle of Mill Bay Woods.

From just behind the Inspector there was a click followed by a strange and electronically generated sound as young James captured the macabre moment using the camera function on his mobile phone.

"I thought that I told you to stay in the car"!

"I went for a wee in the bushes"!

"There exist laws against that sort of thing; and I will have that mobile phone before you Face-Twit the picture........or whatever it is that people of your age do these days when not experimenting with the smoking"! and the Inspector relieved James of his mobile phone.

"My Mum will certainly do for you if I don't get that phone back"!

"Then you will surely have much to talk about later on when you are trying to get even *slightly* comfortable in your mother and son cell; her on the assault charge and you being banged up for urinating in a public place………and that is before we even get onto the theft of the smoking paraphernalia; I take it that you did *steal* the smoking accoutrements and you did not buy them in the village shop; for if it turns out that you *did* buy the tobacco related products in the village shop then I will be duty-bound to close it down"!

"You *are* joking, aren't you; you can't even rent a PG *film* in that shop unless a parent is with you; and it *has* to be a parent………a responsible adult will just not do"!

"I am very glad to hear it; now………why are you not yet back in my car"?

DC Wiseman escorted young James back to their car and he ensured that the child locks were in place before he left the boys on their own again.

"You should really have your siren on"! James shouted after DC Wiseman for the constable had allowed them to wind their windows down.

"You may switch on the flashing lights; but definitely *NO* sirens"!

"A fair compromise"! and the boys switched on the flashing lights and they listened to the chatter on the Police radio.

-4-

By the time that the Inspector and DC Wiseman got to the pub the victorious Welsh team had long since left the field and those still within the Midshipman Bending Over were actively being encouraged to behave themselves for the sake of the Saturday night diners who all looked rather po-faced and not the enjoyers of anything much, let alone rugby; and they were *certainly* not enjoyers of the usual post-match analysis that was still quite on-going.

"Well I *still* say that he's a blooming South African toss-pot"! Steve slurred in relation to the match official. "All right..........we won the game.........but that twat very nearly lost it for us"!

"Those bloody Irish had a sixteen man team with the ref on their side............and we *still* beat 'em"! said Les; who then went back to being quite face down in his bowl of cheesy chips.

"I'm going home for some oysters"! Dave slurred very well. Dave had in fact been regularly announcing his intention to go home for some oysters for the last two hours; but as yet he had not been doing a very good job of actually doing it.

"How about a drop of brandy before you go"? Steve wondered of Dave and by now only one of his eyes was properly functioning. "Will you have a small one with me"?

"Does a shit bear in the woods"?

The pair of detectives took their drinks out to the relative peace and quiet of the smoking area where the Inspector duly sparked up and DC Wiseman didn't.

"Do you know something, Theo; I have lived in this village for the past twenty five years"! and the Inspector was watching the smoke as it drifted away from the end of his cigarette. "It is only a small village and I know pretty much everyone here provided they use the pub or have kids in the school.......but I didn't recognise either of those bodies"!

"Well......they *were* a bit blue and bloated up"! Wiseman reminded his Inspector.

"Be that as it may; if they had been local then I am pretty sure that I would have recognised them"! the Inspector was sure. "So.......the question is this; if they are not local to the village then why dump their bodies here; and why in such bizarre circumstances..............the first body dead before it was strung up in that tree and the second one dead before she got anywhere near that car but with a pipe connected to the exhaust pipe nonetheless. Why on *earth* would somebody go to the trouble of making *both* deaths look like suicides when it is patently obvious that they are not"?

"Perhaps the people involved with the murders are particularly thick"? Wiseman suggested.

"*Nobody* is *that* bloody thick.........that's impossible; no......this is symbolic of something........but symbolic of *what*"? the Inspector mused before he drained his glass and DC Wiseman did a very good job of keeping up with his superior.

"Well; I dare say that we will learn an awful lot more when the bodies have been identified"! DC Wiseman mused aloud as he collected up the empty glasses and he readied himself for a trip to the bar.

"I think I should like a pint of that cloudy cider that they have on draught"! the Inspector elected. "I didn't really go much on that Bishop's whatever it was"!

Chapter Two

A scant six hours later saw DC Wiseman still face down upon the couch in the Inspector's living room; but the young detective was slowly starting to come to......and he was proving himself to be quite accomplished at making the *coming to* noises.

The delicious smell of coffee percolating through from the kitchen was probably helping Wiseman in the waking up department; and only a few moments after Wiseman had identified the smell as being coffee he properly woke up to find his Inspector standing in the door between the kitchen and the living room where he was hurling a multitude of apples, oranges and bananas at him.

"Fresh fruit..............bloody great for a hangover"! the Inspector explained.

"That is very kind, Sir; but I think that I still might be too drunk to have arrived at the hangover stage"! DC Wiseman was reasonably confident. "I hope that *Mrs* Gallant didn't mind me sleeping over on your settee"!

"My good lady is away in Devon visiting her sister as was mentioned to you last night; and you were very welcome to sleep in the spare bedroom, as I *also* mentioned to you last night"!

"You did"?

"Once or twice; and if you are still pissed then *I* had better drive us into the station"!

"It *is* still Sunday..........isn't it"?

"I am sure that a few hours on a Sunday morning won't hurt............provided you don't move your head around unnecessarily; and *we* have a murder board to organise and photographs to start sticking to it"!

"But we won't get very far trying to identify the bodies on a Sunday"! DC Wiseman seemed sure as he stared at the banana that he had just peeled; not sure whether to eat it or to try to zip it back into its skin.

"Precisely; that is why we will only be going in for an hour or so preparatory work; after that we can repair to my local for a nice roast lunch and a few jars while the rugby is on; England against France this afternoon"!

"I am thinking at the moment that I will never touch a drop ever again"!

"You say that *now*; but you have not yet tried some of my specially blended coffee; this stuff will perk you up and have you back on the road to relative normality in no time at all"!

"It smells rather strong, Sir"! Wiseman noticed as he sniffed at the proffered mug.

"It is not for the boys; this really is the kill or cure stuff. Now then.........if I were a set of car keys where would I be"?

"Um...........I don't even know where my *trousers* are at the moment Sir"! Wiseman was honest.

"They are in the tumble drier; you had that accident with the bottle of vodka"!

"Oh yes; little bits of last night are starting to come back to me now; but I thought that it was *tequila* that we were drinking and not vodka"!

"The tequila came first; we both decided to go on the vodka when we finished off the last of my whisky"!

"Ye Gods...........little wonder I am feeling so rough; I never normally touch the spirits.............just one or two pints of beer is my normal routine"!

"Well you were certainly having a bloody good go at them last night. Aha........here are my keys; we shall take my car rather than any of the pool vehicles; that way nobody will know that we are working and we should not be disturbed"!

"Oh.........it didn't rain last night, did it"?

"Not a drop; your backside should not get even *slightly* damp"!

The Inspector's most favoured of personal toys was a shiny and black Jeep Wrangler with a roof that leaked over the passenger seat; and this Jeep he piloted at breakneck speeds through the country lanes as they headed for the main road.

DC Wiseman's mind was presently occupied by holding on firmly to the Inspector's spare coffee machine and the box of specially blended coffee that the Inspector swore as being absolutely essential to any murder investigation until the Police mobile catering van turned up; something that happened during every single murder investigation and quite often when it came to missing persons investigations when the persons being missed were minors.

"We shall spend an hour in the office getting the murder board organised and my spare coffee machine set up; then we shall have a quick look over the little Peugeot that the second body was found in; and then we shall away somewhere for a goodly cooked breakfast before the pub opens its doors"! and the Inspector briefed Wiseman on his plans for the first half of the day.

"And just what the bloody hell is this"? the Inspector wondered as he and Wiseman stood all alone in the upstairs incident room and they looked at the thing in question.

"It is an interactive whiteboard thing"! DC Wiseman seemed sure. "These devices were all the rage when I was in training college"!

"And where are the pins for the affixing of photographs and the like"?

"Um……..you don't *physically stick* the photographs onto one of these, Sir; you upload them from a computer or a memory stick or something like that. You should maybe check your email to see if the shapely Dr Jane Foxy has sent you any pictures of the deceased"!

"The last time I checked my email I had my eleven year old son check it for me; I am a hardworking, hard drinking copper of the old school persuasion; I do not do the checking of email"!

"Would you like me to do it for you"?

"If you would be so kind; and not a word to the Superintendent; this gadgetry is obviously *his* doing and I do not want to appear the twat when it comes to the things technical"!

"Mum shall be the word"!

-3-

"Right; it appears that all we have are *pictures* of the deceased for the time being"! DC Wiseman reported after a few minutes at his Inspector's keyboard; and the images of the deceased appeared as if by magic on their new interactive murder board. "There are some notes underneath.........negative on fingerprints; negative DNA........and get this.........not one single filling or noticeable bit of dental work between them; so the checking of their dental records is probably out as well"!

"What about tattoos..........birthmarks.........scars from previous minor surgery"? the Inspector wondered as he washed up their coffee mugs. "There *must* be something"! the Inspector was sure as he double checked that his coffee machine was all set up ready for first thing the next morning.

"Not according to the shapely Dr Foxy; surely that much is unusual in itself"!

"Right…….first thing in the morning get onto the missing persons lot; until then we shall start the investigation off the old fashioned way……..with a little bit of community policing and the talking to people in and around the village"!

"Yes Sir; I shall go and get my hands on some uniform; although the best we will probably come up with on a Sunday morning are some PCSO's; at least that way we can go door to door with the photographs of the murdered and hideously bloated pair"!

"Do not go forgetting about our cooked breakfasts; after that there is a man in Cosheston who can apparently work wonders with Photoshop or some other digital application; he might be able to tone down the photographs of the deceased a bit for decency's sake; it *is* a Sunday, after all"!

"Would I be correct in assuming that this gentleman of which you know lives in close proximity to the village pub"? DC Wiseman wondered with a grin. The Inspector had been quite right when he promised that his special blend of coffee would sort him out.

"There might be only the matter of a few doors between him and the pub, it is true; and if he is in and we get invited as far as his patio then you would be wise to turn down his offer of a brandy and Baileys combination; you would never make it as far as opening time"! and the Detectives left the Station and they crossed the deserted car park toward the Inspector's Jeep.

"What about the PCSO's; shall I go and see who I can rustle up"?

"No; let's leave the uniformed lot until tomorrow; we should see if we can get the photographs sorted out first"!

"Nigel…….my dear boy; would I be correct in assuming that this would happen to be an *off-duty* visit"? Steve wondered as he opened the door to the two detectives.

"As it happens we are both very *off-duty* for the rest of the day"! the Inspector told the Steve who was very locally renowned for his rugby commentary *and* his Photoshop abilities.

"Then please come through to the patio; my wife is away playing golf so we shall not be disturbed or even nagged to any great extent. Would you both care for some tea or coffee……….or maybe something a little stronger"?

"As long as what you have in mind is no stronger than beer; Wiseman and I have some casual investigating to do a little later on and we thought that we might do that when the match is on in the pub; that is usually a good time to catch a good cross section of the community"!

"Then I should start work on these photographs; I must say that you were rather secretive when you were on the telephone. Make yourselves at home while I go and grab my laptop"!

Steve returned with his laptop computer and a whole case of bottled beer that he had dragged from his garage and he set to work on the photographs that DC Wiseman had saved onto a memory stick.

"What do you think"? Steve wondered only a few minutes later. "This latest edition of Photoshop is absolutely phenomenal"!

"Granted..........they *do* look a lot less blue and bloated; but I do not recall either of them having such huge manes of cascading blonde locks"!

"I thought that it might make them look a bit more realistic"!

"Um.........if you could just lose the hair and the bright red trout-pouts then that will be just what we were looking for"! and DI Gallant was as diplomatic as he could be when his beer bottle was almost empty.

"Not a problem; now then..........what about the background; I've got a few shots of the Grand Canyon that I could squeeze in there; maybe a few boulders in the foreground to lead the eye into the photograph"?

"Just the slabs that they are lying upon will be fine; and thank you for your help………and the lovely beer"!

"My pleasure; and please help yourselves to some more while I just nip upstairs and print these out; and by the time that I am done the Midshipman will be open for trade and you would do well to consider conducting some of your enquiries in there; somebody might well have seen these people knocking around the village when they were still very much alive"!

"Why don't you walk down to the pub with us"? the Inspector wondered only a few minutes later when Steve returned down the stairs with the printed out photographs.

"Just give me a few minutes to get Sunday lunch on the go"!

"Okay; I'm ready"! Steve announced not thirty seconds later as he disposed of the empty supermarket bags that once contained the ready prepared vegetables that now sat in pans of water upon the kitchen table all ready to be boiled.

"What have you got then"?

"Carrots, peas and green beans; roast and boiled"!

"Meat wise"?

"Roast pork with the magic crackling that never fails; two and a half hours from freezer to table"!

"You seem to have everything organised"!

"Piece of piss………shall we"? and Steve motioned himself and the detectives toward his front door.

-5-

Even though it was only five minutes after midday the bar of the Midshipman soon became very full of customers; mostly male and all of them seeing just how many pints they could sling down in the scant hour before their various roast dinners were placed upon their various tables. The only exception to the Sunday norm was Dave, whose wife was playing golf with Steve's wife; and once again it was Dave's intention to have one or two drinks only and then to go home and eat the oysters that he didn't eat yesterday on the grounds of diminished responsibility.

"Is that photo admissible as evidence now that it has quite obviously been Photo-shopped"? Dave wondered with a wry smile and a little gesture that demonstrated just how empty his pint glass was.

"The unadulterated original might well have put you off your Sunday lunch"! DC Wiseman explained.

"Nothing puts me off oysters"! Dave was sure.

"Have you seen either of these people in the village before"! DC Wiseman asked him again.

"Should you be drinking that pint if you are on duty"?

"Technically I am not *on* duty; this is what we call *casual Policing*"!

"That's the trouble with the world today; everything is far too casual"!

"So………have you seen either of these people before"?

"I don't know………I haven't got my glasses"!

"Ye Gods"! Wiseman muttered under his breath as he made up his mind to go and casually Police at the other end of the bar.

"Here you are Dave……..have the pub glasses" and the Inspector handed to Dave the spectacles that were lost property but which everybody used until such a day as they might be reclaimed by their rightful owner.

"You should have a word with Steve; he could give these people some hair……..make them look alive again"!

"So………do the faces ring any bells"? the Inspector wondered as he passed a fresh pint to Dave.

"Not the fella……..I am sure that I have never seen him before; but the woman……….she *does* seem sort of familiar; maybe I have seen her in a shop somewhere; or maybe behind the bar in a different pub"?

"Well; if you have a brainwave and you suddenly remember where you have seen her before then perhaps you could give either myself or Wiseman a ring" and the Inspector handed over his Police calling card.

"I don't think that you can use the term *brainwave* anymore; it implies that those who are too thick to have them are somewhat lacking..........which of course they are. Right; time for one more then I am *definitely* away for my oysters"!

"Thank you for your time"! DC Wiseman was polite; but he was quite relieved to get away from that table.

"Did you get on any better Sir"? Wiseman wondered of his Inspector.

"No; one or two maybe's, but they can't really be sure; and there probably won't be many more locals coming in now because the England game is on bloody Sky and the pub doesn't have it; so..........we might as well order some lunch. Have you shown the photo's to the barmaid; she probably sees a lot of faces coming and going"!

"I have spoken to her before, Sir; and if I remember rightly she has only recently moved here from Cardiff or Newport or somewhere like that; she probably won't know that many people from down here"!

"Who is to say that the victims *are* from down here........I certainly didn't recognise them; get chatting to her; she is a very pretty girl...........you might even get lucky"!

"Yes Sir"!

"Dynamite, Guv"!

"Please do not call me that"!

"Sorry Sir; dynamite Sir"!

"And what is dynamite, Wiseman"?

"Well..........not only did I manage to get a date with the barmaid.........but she thinks that she knows our female victim as well"!

"At last; so who is she then"?

"Well; she thinks that she knows her *slightly*; she doesn't know her name or anything but she knows in which circles she used to move"!

"And what circles would they be"?

"Salsa dancing; the barmaid thinks that she saw her at a recent salsa dancing congress in Swansea"!

"Salsa………..that's all tight trousers and shouting *olé* a lot, isn't it"?

"Actually Sir I think that's Flamenco………..but you're close enough"!

"Right then; first thing tomorrow morning, after you have liaised with the missing person's lot, get these photo's over to South Wales Police and see if they can shed any light on the subject. As for now, I am going to have the beef……….they do it properly medium-rare here; how about you"?

"Two beef then"!

Chapter Three

The Inspector arrived at the Station at a very overly punctual six of the horribly early morning clock; very nearly frightening the poor old Desk Sergeant into an early grave; and he wasted no time in setting about with the preheating of his spare coffee machine and the warming up in the microwave of his favourite mug.

He passed a cursory glance at the new and interactive murder board and he tutted because he could not stick anything to said board or even look at it in a detective-like way until DC Wiseman arrived and turned it on; and that was probably at least an hour away.

"Any developments worth speaking of"?

It was the Superintendent who had poked his head around the door to the incident room.

"Well; yes and no Sir"! the Inspector was honest. The Inspector explained all about the lack of any ID about the bodies of *both* of the deceased; and also about the lack of any DNA or dental records or fingerprints on any of the databases that might have proved helpful; and he was about to relate to the Super about how DC Wiseman had unearthed a possible connection to the salsa dancing fraternity of Swansea when the Superintendent stopped him.

"My *God* that coffee smells good"! and Superintendent Bell ceased with just poking his head around the door and he walked into the incident room. "That doesn't smell like any of your common or garden supermarket coffee; special blend, is it"?

"It is blended especially to my tastes; and you would be very welcome to a cup……..although I should warn you that this particular blend does seem somewhat stronger than usual"!

"You know me………I am no coffee virgin; bring it on"! the Superintendent was sure. "Would you also happen to have any of the little continental biscuits that might go well with it"?

By the time that DC Wiseman arrived at the Station the Superintendent had eyes the size of dish-plates and he was telling the Inspector all about the internal workings of the new and interactive murder board and all about how jolly good it was……..and the Superintendent was telling the Inspector this much very quickly; very quickly indeed; *so* quickly, in fact, that his sentences were all running together and the start of a new sentence was not easily discernible from the end of the one before it; sort of like the ramblings of a hyperactive drunk.

The detectives left the Superintendent to his drug-induced ramblings and they retreated to the Inspector's office.

"I will email the photographs to South Wales Police right now……….if you do not mind me using your computer"? and DC Wiseman took a big swig of the coffee that by now he was more or less used to. "I don't rightly know how long it will take for them to get back to us"?

"Before the Super succumbed to the caffeine onslaught he sounded quite keen for both of us to do some of the old fashioned Policing; knocking upon people's doors and the like"! the Inspector explained.

"But will we learn anything that we didn't already glean from the locals in the pub yesterday afternoon"?

"Quite possibly; for one.......yesterday none of the wives were present in the pub and they are generally the more observant; secondly, and more to the point, the pub doesn't open of a Monday lunchtime and so those we catch at home we stand a good chance of finding relatively sober if we are early enough in the day"!

"And when we get back we might well have had a reply from South Wales Police"! DC Wiseman was hopeful.

"Between you and me there should be a lovely little something waiting for *both of* us at the Station when we get back"! the Inspector said with a smile.

"What would that be, Sir"?

"Well; because we are now investigating a double murder, Headquarters are sending down their mobile catering unit; I can almost taste those freshly cooked bacon sandwiches. I know that this is just an attempt to get us to spend more time at the Station during our lunch breaks and everything........but to be honest I just don't bloody care. Right; you can drive..........they are forecasting the possibility of showers later on and I have left the Jeep in the garage; but before we go anywhere I would like you to assemble uniform in the briefing room; I will be there to go over exactly what is required of them after I have just nipped outside for a quick smoke"!

The Inspector was grinding his cigarette stub into the asphalt of the Station's car park when a sudden squealing of tyres caused him to spin around.

The large and black van had seemingly appeared from nowhere and its front bumper stopped mere inches from the Inspector's knees.

"If you are the mobile catering unit then please allow the cholesterol in your bacon sandwiches to kill me rather than trying to do it with your van"!

The side door to the van slid open and the Inspector was dragged within where he had a sack wrestled over his head.

"Do you know who I am; I will see you doing time for this"! the Inspector assured his captor or captors very loudly before he was hit upon the back of his head with something rather heavy and blunt; and not even the sheer amount of pure caffeine that was coursing through the Inspector's veins could prevent him from passing out.

-4-

When the Inspector awoke he found that he had been sat upon a deckchair and that the deckchair itself was sitting upon a bare and rocky outcrop that was overlooking a huge and sandy desert the likes of the Kalahari or similar; or so the Inspector was thinking.

Windblown sand blasted painfully at the exposed skin of his face; save for where the gag gad been placed and the sunglasses had been positioned; and after a few attempts at the scratching of his itching nose the Inspector realised that his hands were bound behind his back and also behind the back of the deckchair.

The unmistakable route of a long since dried up river bed still meandered and snaked through the lowest point of the desert valley; and in the distance the skeletal remains of no doubt once-busy jetties lay twisted and warped looking in the heat haze of the sun-baked land.

"It probably doesn't look too familiar"! said the rather mechanical sounding voice whose point of origin was somewhere behind the Inspector and his deckchair.

"Holy shit; I have been kidnapped by Stephen bloody Hawking"! the Inspector barked; for try as he might he could not turn very far in his canvas seat to face the voice that was now speaking to him. "That bloody wheelchair of yours is going to be up your own bloody arse if you do not untie me pretty bloody quickly"!

"My voice has been digitally disguised for security reasons; and what you see before you is what is left of the lower Cleddau Estuary……..the very river that used to run past your house. If you look very carefully at what used to be downstream you will see the remnants of the old Valero and LNG jetties"!

"This is quite obviously a desert, you simpleminded oaf"! the Detective was sure and so he said as much. "Where have you taken me; those back at the Station will not rest until they have found me"!

"On the contrary; your colleagues back at the Station will not even have noticed that you have gone; and as to *where* we have taken you………..the question better asked would be to *when* we have taken you; this, Inspector, is your future……..or at least one of your *possible* futures; we hope that you do not like it too much"!

"Aha………..*now* I understand it; this is indeed a very well painted canvas backdrop and you will be one of the many crack-head artists that I will have nicked before now. Untie me this very minute, Rembrandt………..and I will put in a good word for you; you will probably end up with smacked wrists and a few hours of community service painting graffiti with gypsy kids"!

"Were it that easy, Inspector Gallant......" and the person who had been doing most of the talking up until now moved from behind the deckchair and he took to standing right in front of it. The Inspector clapped eyes upon a man, or what he assumed to be a man; a person who was dressed from head to toe entirely in black, with a black ski-mask and very dark sunglasses occupying his head.

"I will prove to you that this is no canvas backdrop"! and the Inspector was lifted from his deckchair, turned around and then marched back toward the big and black van that had very nearly done for him in the car park at the Police Station.

The Inspector was helped into the passenger seat and the masked man took his place behind the wheel; and from the rocky outcrop they drove down a large sand dune, across the dried up bed of what his captor would have the Inspector believe was once the Cleddau River; and then up the sand dune on the other side.

And it was as they were driving up the sand dune on the other side of the supposedly dried up river bed that things started becoming slightly familiar to the Inspector. They turned off the main sand dune and onto a track between two very much smaller dunes; but the Inspector knew that a silvered road lay beneath the sand because of the noise that the van's tyres were making. The two very much smaller dunes on either side of the track served as hedgerows of a kind; but the Inspector was suddenly reminded of the occasional journeys that he used to make when there was snow on the ground……..the more normal hedgerows not easily recognisable but familiar all the same. And then the van pulled abruptly off that track and headed down an even narrower lane; still covered in sand and yet still asphalt beneath; and the Inspector breathed in automatically as the van came perilously close to side-swiping and old and rusted gate that was hanging half off its hinges; a gate which bore the nameplate Valhalla; Valhalla………*his* house; *his* gatepost; and he recognised more of the lay of the land as the van travelled along *his* driveway and toward the ruins of a once great house.

"Any of this ringing a bell *now*"? the masked driver asked of the Inspector.

"What the bloody hell is this"?

"This, my friend, is fifty years into your most likely future and you have a lot of work to do. Now then………..let us start with the most recent of occurrences and the body of the man that you had to cut down from the tree……."!

Chapter Four

"Ladies and gentlemen..........I do humbly apologise if I am at all tardy and have kept you waiting"! the Inspector apologised as he entered the briefing room.

"Um..........if anything Sir, you are early; I thought that you were going for a cigarette"! DC Wiseman looked confused. "And there is dried blood around your left earhole and you seem to be leaving a trail of sand behind you..........Sir"! Wiseman *also* noticed.

The Inspector chose to ignore DC Wiseman for the immediate time being and instead he turned his attention to the briefing room full of uniformed constables who had been attached to the murder investigation.

"Constables; you have your photographs........and actually they would *not* look more realistic with a bit of hair. Please begin with your door to door enquiries and use your pocket books to record *everything* that is said to you and by whom…….no matter *how* inconsequential you think it at the time. Now then; who among you have been allocated the task of knocking upon the doors in the estate known as Westhaven"?

"That would be myself and PC Turner"! PC Parker told the Inspector.

"Right; do not bother yourselves with houses one, two and three; DC Wiseman and myself will knock upon those particular doors……..everywhere else is fair game. Does anybody have any questions"?

The room fell quiet and DC Wiseman sent the constables upon their various ways while the Inspector helped himself to another dose of his special coffee.

"Wiseman………you have drunk the same amount of coffee as have I this morning"! and Wiseman knew the Inspector well enough to know that there was something that he wished to get off his chest. "You haven't experienced any strange visions or anything, have you"?

"Visions Sir………no Sir; a slight tightening of the chest……but none of the visions; visions I would have noticed. What is it, Sir; has the Super been at your coffee again. The last time this happened we had to release a load of apprehended druggies because the Super *ate* the evidence"!

"No; the Super *has* had some coffee but he seems to be just fine; it's just………oh, nothing really; forget about it. Now then; when we get to number three Westhaven you make sure that you have all of your wits about you and listen to every word that is said to us and also think about the words that are *not* spoken; and have as much of a scout around as you can"!

"Have you had a tip-off or something"?

"Something along those lines; now……..be a good man and nip down the stairs and see if the mobile catering unit has turned up yet while I wash the blood from my earhole and empty the sand from my pockets"!

The mobile catering unit had indeed arrived but needed certain amount of time before any food suitable for consumption could be produced and so the detectives set off on the road to Cosheston; the only thing within their stomachs the Inspector's rather potent coffee.

"Which house do you want to take first then"? DC Wiseman wondered as they sat in their unmarked car at the bottom of the Westhaven estate.

"Not one of them at the time being"! the Inspector replied after thinking long and hard about it for a goodly minute. "Before we start with the ringing of any bells especially the *alarm* bells I think that it might be pertinent to find out just what these people get up to after dark"!

"Come again Sir"?

"Wiseman.........when was the last time you rode a bicycle"?

The detectives hung around with their uniformed colleagues until five of the afternoon clock which was pretty much the time of the change of shift and also the end of the door to door enquiries for that particular day; and with Wiseman at the wheel they drove through the village and down toward the river and the home of Detective Inspector Gallant.

"Just take a look at *them* apples"! the Inspector rhetorically asked of DC Wiseman as they stood within his double garage.

"In the years that I have known you I never had you down as the mountain biking type"! Wiseman was honest.

"Isn't she a beauty; I have virtually built her myself"! the Inspector said very proudly. "Giant frame; Marzocchi front forks; Fox rear shock; race-face crank; Sunline bars; Saint derailleur.......and about two hundred gears"! and the Inspector was still fairly gushing when it came to his wonderful mountain bike.

"Very nice indeed Sir; but is there a point to all of this"?

"There is *always* a point, DC Wiseman; in this instance I am expecting some rather peculiar nocturnal goings on…….and quite possibly tonight; and if we try to tail those involved in your car then they will surely notice our presence……..what with this being a smallish village and it being rather late at night; so we shall conduct our enquiries on bicycles instead"!

"Would there be one for me Sir"?

"You can use the wife's bike"! and the Inspector pointed it out.

"But that is obviously a ladies bike with the funny crossbar and everything"! and DC Wiseman sounded rather put out. "And you cannot get away from the fact that it is bright pink"!

"I am afraid that there is only that one"!

"What about that bicycle in the corner"?

"What; my eleven year old son's BMX stunt bike"?

"It seems quite a tall bike; and I am not that long in the leg; I should like to take that one if it is all the same"!

"I am sure that Rory would not mind. Now then; it is fast approaching six of the evening clock and the Midshipman is soon to open. We should get ourselves up there and have a drink and send out for some Chinese or Indian or something; when it is delivered we shall bring it back here because those delivery people can never find my house; and by the time that dinner is done and dusted it will be time to get ourselves in position"!

"Get ourselves in position for *what*, exactly"?

"You will see……..I think; in a few hours I am hoping that we *both* see a lot more than we bargained for"!

-4-

"Slow down Sir; I have but the one gear"! DC Wiseman pleaded as he endeavoured to keep up with the Inspector as they cycled up the long and quite steep hill that led away from the old ferry house.

"You should have used the wife's bike as was my suggestion; twenty-seven gears on that baby and she's as light as a feather"!

"And also very pink"!

"Wiseman……….it is eleven o'clock and as black as it should be out here; who is going to see what colour your bike is"?

"In hindsight you make a very good point"!

The Inspector waited at the top of the hill for Wiseman to catch him up; and he lit a cigarette as he listened to Wiseman wheezing his last as he furiously pedalled the stunt BMX bike.

At the top of the hill where the silvered road turned sharply right and headed toward the village they were faced with three gravel tracks. The first track headed down to Bank Farm where trespassers and sales agents would not be tolerated, as the hand written sign clearly stated. The middle track was not signposted or labelled in any way, but it was not where they wanted to go. Instead the Inspector led Wiseman along the right hand gravel track that had signs that advised of its private nature.

"Right then Wiseman; what do you make of that first house up there on the right"?

"It looks a bit churchy"! Wiseman was sure in between puffs.

"Very good that man; it is an old chapel as it happens…….but you are close enough; and in the field behind the chapel is where I have been assured it will all be happening. We should push the bikes from here and hide behind those trees over there on that far ridge. What time do you have"?

"Quarter past eleven Sir"!

"I have a feeling that our guests will be arriving fairly soon; but we still have plenty of time to conceal ourselves; and we shall have to steer well clear of the old chapel………..the owners of the property have two dogs who will surely howl like banshees if disturbed"!

"This had better be worth it Sir; those sweet and sour king prawns are now sitting very heavily upon my stomach"!

"I hope that what you are about to see doesn't make you bring your Chinese banquet back up"!

"Sir, look over there..........lights in the distance; car headlights by the look of it.......and heading this way"! and DC Wiseman pointed out what the Inspector had already noticed some minutes ago.

"Yes; four cars by my estimation; and the lights in the old chapel have just come on"!

"It is a good job that the moon is now full otherwise we might well have found ourselves sitting here in the dark"! Wiseman was sure.

"It is *because* the moon is full that we are finding ourselves here. Now.........be very quiet and we will just observe what is going on for the time being"!

The four cars pulled into the bottom end of the paddock behind the old chapel and parked up next to one another; and the occupants all climbed out. Voices could be heard on the gentle breeze; but too far away to be understood. At the same time that the conversations were too far away to be heard they were also only just about recognisable as being human on account of the long robes with their enormous cowls that they were all wearing.

"What time have you got"? the Inspector whispered.

"Quarter to twelve; what the hell are they all doing out here at this time of night"?

The twelve occupants of the cars were joined by two more robed persons from the old chapel and together they all made their ways to the centre of the paddock.

One of the robed individuals placed a lantern upon the stump of a long since removed tree and they all joined hands and stared up at the full moon; the soft voices of the women among them drifting through the night air as they muttered some form of incantation.

"Bloody hell, they are chanting something or other…….are these Devil worshippers or something"? Wiseman whispered.

"*Something* would be my guess"! the Inspector whispered back.

Just after the Inspector had finished with his whispering one of the robed mob, and it was the voice of a *man* this time, declared that it was midnight and that the witching hour was upon them; at which point they all dropped their hoods and then their robes and they proceeded to dance around and frolic whilst quite naked.

"Get a load of all that; they are starkers........every single one of them"! Wiseman almost giggled like a schoolboy but the Inspector managed to clamp a hand over his mouth just in time.

"What are they doing"? Wiseman managed to whisper just as soon as the Inspector had released his mouth from his vice-like grip. "If this lot are Devil worshippers then perhaps they are trying to raise Behemoth or something"?

"These are not Devil worshippers Wiseman; these are *witches*"! the Inspector revealed with a wry smile. "It would seem that the quite little village of Cosheston has its very own Coven"!

"But I thought that the witches of this modern day were all herbal piles remedies and clothes pegs"! Wiseman seemed sure.

"No; that's the gypsies. Now; I am no expert on the occult by *any* means…………but I think that there probably exists a difference between the white witches and the black ones; and that frolicking around at midnight whilst quite starkers is more than likely a *black* witch thing; but apart from public indecency and a few other public order offences there doesn't seem anything much to nab them for……and no reason to either"!

"What if they start sacrificing lambs or kittens or something"?

"Now that really *is* Devil worship; but these are definitely not the Devil worshippers"!

"So; apart from the frolicking around whilst quite naked, what is it that these witches get up to; and why get up to it all the way out here"?

"I don't honestly know……….yet. This might be an ideal spot for their frolicking because it is so out of the way and the owners of the old chapel are obviously members of the Coven as well; or it could be that this land, as belonging to the old chapel, is consecrated or something and they need that connection for their witchcraft business. This is a professional first for me; and it is all stuff that we will have to find out…….so thank goodness for Google; but now we know what it is that they are up to I think it fairly safe to say that we now have an ace up *our* sleeves"!

"But they are wearing masks and they are quite a long way away; we don't have any idea of who these people are"!

"Then we shall leave our bicycles chained to this tree and we shall very quietly creep around the edge of the field and take down the details of their number plates. Then, first thing tomorrow morning while we are waiting for my spare coffee machine to warm up we can run the plates and get some ID"!

"Do you think that these weirdoes are in any way connected with the murders"?

"Too early to say; but it does seem a very good place to start with our investigation"!

Chapter Five

"Three of the cars are registered as being legally kept in Cosheston; and one is from Pembroke Dock…….those must be the *travelling* weirdoes"! DC Wiseman announced as the Inspector sipped on his coffee and he handed a second mug to the young Detective Constable. "And these are all well respected people; a few consultants………some high level brass from the local County Council and a doctor of marine biology"!

"I expected nothing less; they do call it *posh-Cosh* you know"!

"So where do we start"?

The Inspector shuffled through the small pile of papers that DC Wiseman had handed to him; and he moved just one sheet of paper to the top of the pile.

"We shall start with this one!" and the Inspector handed the papers back to DC Wiseman.

"Any particular reason Sir"?

"Call it a Copper's hunch; and also it is the furthest house from the pub and we shall work through the village from west to east until we get close to opening time; there are a few things that I would speak with the landlord about"!

"It doesn't look as if anybody is at home; which is not unusual for two professional people"! Wiseman concluded after a few minutes of knocking upon the door and ringing at the bell. "We could always try another house on our list and come back later"!

"We should try the back door first"!

The back garden was tidy and well-tended and dominated by a hot-tub; and the detectives skirted around this and they approached the patio doors. Wiseman peered in; his hands cupped and his breath misting the glass.

"No signs of life in there; I am telling you, Sir......they are both at work"!

"Ah..........but just look at this"! and the Inspector was now examining the back door; that quite possibly led to a kitchen; the top half of the door being made up of small glass panels. The Inspector's elbow smashed the pane of glass that was nearest to the door handle and he reached in and turned the key in the lock.

"Clear evidence of an aggravated entry"! the Inspector said with a grin. "We are duty-bound to investigate"!

"I *hate* it when you do that"!

The back door did indeed lead into a kitchen; but it was via a utility room with a chest freezer humming away in its corner; a washing machine and a tumble drier. To the side of the washing machine was a tall raffia basket for the keeping of laundry; and the Inspector fished around in the basket; eventually pulling out two hooded robes of exactly the same type as they had seen being worn only the night before; right up until the naked frolicking had started.

"We now know that the occupants of this house will be lying if they claim that their car was borrowed last night; or mysteriously stolen without them realising"! the Inspector said with yet another of his grins that stretched from ear to ear. "Ring the Station and ask them to get onto the lady of the house and inform her of the aggravated entry; we shall wait here for her lest the miscreants return and then we can take a statement once she has had a look around and decided if anything's missing; which we know will not be the case if she is anything but honest. In the meantime we shall have a little shifty around; I do not think that these people are in any way connected to the murders.........but up until last night I wasn't even aware that Cosheston has its own witches Coven; who knows *what* we might drag up"!

The Inspector put the robes back into the raffia laundry basket; and then he pulled them back out again and he had another look at them.

"There are name tags sewn into these robes"! he informed DC Wiseman. "Granny and……..Manbooba"! the Inspector read aloud. "They must be witch names within the Coven; curiouser and curiouser"! and the Inspector once again buried the robes at the bottom of the laundry basket where he had found them and he followed Wiseman into the kitchen itself.

An interior wall had been knocked down at one stage which meant that the kitchen was now at the end of a long and very smart living room; the other end of the living space being occupied with a three piece suite and a thirty-six inch plasma screen TV. The Inspector walked passed these and into the hallway and front door where that morning's post was still lying; and then something that was half way up the stairs grabbed his attention.

"I have rung the Station Sir; they are going to ring the householder straight away"! DC Wiseman informed the Inspector as he met up with him in the hallway.

"What do you make of *that*"? and the Inspector pointed.

"That would be a cat Sir"! and DC Wiseman was not going to be fooled easily.

"But it is a very big and *black* cat"! the Inspector added.

"It has white bits on its legs"! Wiseman noticed.

"But it is *mostly* black………..just like a witch's familiar. I placed my foot upon the bottom riser as if to go upstairs and that cat hissed and spat at me"!

"Fur balls"? Wiseman wondered; and when he saw the look upon the Inspector's face he quickly got the conversation moving again. "Why do witches have the familiars anyway"?

"Well, like I said…….I am no expert on the occult; but I think that witches believe that minor spirits and the like can take on the form of a small animal such as a cat and said animal can help the witch about her business; maybe acting as some sort of spy"!

"Well; if that cat *is* a spy then it will surely grass us up for breaking and entering"! Wiseman was sure. "Why did you want to go upstairs anyway; we haven't properly finished poking around *downstairs* yet. I have it Sir………….you're looking for a broomstick, aren't you"?

"Maybe I am; or maybe it was a *computer* that I was looking for. These are both professional people and yet there is no computer in the living room"! the Inspector pointed out. "Maybe you could distract the cat and I can sneak past"!

But before either of them could go sneaking off anywhere there was the sound of a car as it pulled into the drive and the detectives quickly headed back into the kitchen.

A rather lovely looking Audi convertible was now parked on the driveway and a sun-bronzed female was clacking toward the house upon the highest of heels. The Inspector opened the back kitchen door for her and with a smile he introduced himself and DC Wiseman and he beckoned the woman into her own home.

"In a world of austerity and cutbacks can the Dyfed Powys Police really spare two members of CID for a simple case of breaking and entering"? Mrs Mills wondered as she put the kettle on. At the Inspector's behest she had already had a good look around and she was satisfied that nothing had been misappropriated.

"We were already in the area conducting enquiries into the more macabre events of the weekend"! and the Inspector was selectively honest. "Our Superintendent thought it only polite for us to wait here until you had been notified"!

The friend of a friend of Mrs Mills was already replacing the broken glass panel in the back door and that cat had moved from the stairs to perching atop the laundry basket where he eyed the detectives and the handyman alike with equal distrust. The Inspector reached across the table to snaffle a few of the digestives and the cat immediately sprang to its feet and arched its back and spat as hissed at everybody.

"Quiet now Wicksy"! Mrs Mills urged her cat. "He is always this off with strangers; we rescued him, you know".

"He is adorable"! the Inspector lied. "That is an unusual name; are you a fan or Eastenders"?

"I can't remember *where* the name Wicksy came from; probably down to one of the grandchildren; he was a Sammy when we first got him but I don't think that it really suited him; he's been Wicksy ever since"!

"Well; thank you for the coffee Mrs Mills; and thank you also for your time; as for now DC Wiseman and myself had better get back to the nasty business in hand"! and the Inspector stood up to leave.

"A thoroughly nasty business that"! said Mrs Mills. "Have you got anything to go on yet"?

"We are following up a few leads; we shall of course keep the local residents informed but as the victims were not from around here I do not think that anybody in the village has anything to worry about"!

"What about my break in; do you think that the two are related"?

"Um……..I don't wish to speak out of turn but the broken glass is a bit oily in places"! the handyman told them. "I reckon a bird like a pigeon or something has flown into it and broken it"!

"That much has happened to me before now"! the Inspector lied. "Good day Mrs Mills"!

"Wicksy…….."! the Inspector said as they climbed back into their unmarked car. "That sounds more than a little bit like Wicca………..and *that* is the Old English word for *witch*"! the Inspector explained. "I wonder if these familiars are passed around; even before he was Wicksy he was called Sammy.......and *that* could have been derived from Samhain which is the beginning of the Celtic New Year; suddenly there are Pagan connections everywhere"!

"Where to now Sir; shall we try the house next door"?

"No; back to the Station for a bacon sarnie and a cup of decent coffee; I just don't see the point in drinking that decaffeinated stuff that we have recently had to endure; it is like alcohol free wine...........where is the point or the *taste* in that"?

-3-

"This is what I wanted you to see"! said the shapely Dr Foxy and she produced a number of photographs as she, the Inspector and DC Wiseman all sat around the Inspector's desk; munching upon bacon sandwiches and swigging black coffee. "There is quite extensive bruising across the lower torsos of each of the bodies; and bruising patterns consistent with having a hand pushing down upon the backs of their heads"!

"And that would mean"? the Inspector wondered in between mouthfuls of delectable and crispy bacon.

"That they were probably forcibly held over a large barrel or water butt until they were dead. Can I have another squeeze of your ketchup"?

"Not a nice way to go; do we have any identification yet"?

"Not as yet; but the analysis of their stomach contents suggests to me that they are not British; or if they *were* British then they had very cosmopolitan diets. No; I am thinking that they might have been German or maybe Austrian.......or from that part of the world *somewhere*"!

"Aha..........I know that there is a German company presently very interested in buying land in Cosheston to set up a huge solar panel park affair; everything is still in the planning stages at the moment but quite a few of the residents of Cosheston are quite up in arms about it and are kicking up a bit of a fuss"! the Inspector remembered. "Wiseman; find out who this German company is and see if they have any members of a survey team or something gone missing. I will get onto County

Hall and see if a petition against the solar park thing has been handed in; I know that there was one doing the rounds and it might be handy to see just whose names are on there"!

"Sir"!

"Sir; I think that we might be getting somewhere"! DC Wiseman sounded optimistic. "The German company behind the application for the solar park have become worried about two of their employees who have suddenly gone missing………a Günter Van Rhyn and a Nicola Von Hooper. The director of the survey side of the company is based in Wales and he knows these two individuals well; he is prepared to identify the bodies and is travelling down from Cardiff as we speak"!

"Excellent work, Wiseman; *now* we finally seem to be getting somewhere; if the identification of the bodies is positive then at least we will know what they were doing in the village; but is the siting of a solar park cause enough to get them both killed"?

"Perhaps those wind farmers are behind it"? Wiseman suggested. "They have had a lot of bad press lately; ever since that turbine in Scotland blew up because it was a little bit too windy. There is a place just down the road that manufactures the wind turbines; perhaps a solar park right under their very noses in windy West Wales might well be the final straw as far as they are concerned"!

"Wiseman………you are on fire; get onto Company's House in Cardiff………see who is behind the wind turbine people; and then we can have a quick lunch before this German fella arrives"!

"I have heard that the Ferry Inn is doing Mexican food all this week" DC Wiseman suggested.

"I do love the Mexican food, as you know; but I am not stepping foot in that place again; it is all loud sofas and cheap tat; it is like sitting inside the twee gypsy caravan of old"!

"Fair point; the Shipwright's then"?

"No; let us go and roll the dice in the First and Last; I feel more like a sandwich than anything cooked and the First and Last is just over the road from the industrial estate that houses the

windmill people. If we listen carefully we might hear some

tongues-a-wagging"!

Chapter Six

-1-

"There is just not enough bloody justice in this world"! the Inspector was sure. "That will be twice now that you have rolled the dice and have got a free pint when it is your turn in the chair; and twice now that I have won bugger all. Now.........is this a case of the sun shining on the righteous or the Devil looking after his own"?

"Um..........what with all of the recent goings on in Cosheston I would be happy if you didn't speak of the Devil at all"! DC Wiseman protested. "I don't pretend to know much about the occult either; but I feel sure that the Devil is involved somewhere along the line"!

"I don't know as much; I think that the goings on of last night are less of the occult and more of an excuse for some outdoor kinky sex"! the Inspector reassured Wiseman. "What is the latest on that German fella travelling down from Cardiff"?

"I had a text message from him about ten minutes ago saying that he was about twenty minutes away; he should be here any minute now"!

"What.........*here* in this very pub"?

"Yes Sir; the gentleman's name is Roy Greenslade and he will be meeting us here directly"!

"Roy Greenslade...........he doesn't sound particularly German, does he"?

"He isn't Sir; he is a valley's boy who just happens to work for the German solar panel company. He knows the area well because he has worked down here many times before; and when I mentioned that we were having some lunch in the First and Last he jumped at the chance to meet us here"!

"I think that I like the sound of this Roy Greenslade already; and I am thinking that maybe I should wait out the back in the smoking shelter for him; he will have to walk past the smoke shack to get in the back door"!

"I will come with you Sir; I have arrested many of the younger element in this pub and I am starting to get some menacing looks"!

"Now *there* is something that you don't see every day in Pembroke Dock"!

"What is that Sir"?

"A Porsche in the car park; and a Porsche 911 Turbo at that and not one of those Boxster training Porsche's"!

"Perhaps it is the landlord's"?

"No; his is the Evo over there in the corner; don't you just love the lines on a Porsche like this"? and the Inspector left the smoking shelter and he started across the car park to where the Porsche was parked.

"I am not altogether sure of the banana yellow paint job"! Wiseman was honest. "I think that a *red* Porsche looks a lot nicer; or a black one"!

"It certainly is cheerful"!

It wasn't until they had walked a bit closer that they realised that there was somebody sitting in the driver's seat; and not until they got closer still that Wiseman noticed the small hole at the top of the windscreen; and then they both noticed that whatever had pierced the windscreen had also entered the driver's head, opening up a much bigger hole before passing out the back of the driver's head, taking most of the back of his skull with it and leaving a right old mess of blood and bone and brain matter all over the lovely headrest"!

"Bloody hell………..that is Mr Greenslade"! and DC Wiseman pointed at the remains.

"How so sure; I thought that you had only spoken to him on the telephone"!

"I looked him up on his company website after I spoke to him for the first time and thought that he didn't sound particularly German"!

"Is this whole town going bloody crazy"? the Inspector wondered quite loudly. "Right; get on the phone; we will be needing scenes of crime again and that means that we might as well head back to the station after they turn up to await the results………and tell them from me that I want the briefcase that is on the passenger seat at the first possible instance"!

By the time that the Inspector and DC Wiseman entered the Station armed with their crispy bacon baguettes and two portions of hot'n'spicy chicken wings the briefcase belonging to the late Roy Greenslade was already waiting for them on the Inspector's desk.

"You are *really* going to hate me for this"! the very shapely Dr Foxy promised the Inspector as she sat in the comfy chair in the corner of the Inspector's office.

"So………..it was *you* that had the last portion of chips"!

"No……….not that; it's Mr Greenslade…….he didn't die in his car"!

"Yes he did; there were brains and bone and all *manner* of head gunk all over the seat of his car"! and DC Wiseman argued the toss as he tucked into his chicken wings.

"He was shot in the head whilst sitting in his car……yes; but Mr Greenslade was already dead by then"!

"Drowned"?

"No; strangled this time; and based on the trajectory of the bullet the car could not have been in the car park of the First and Last when the shooting occurred; there are no points high enough for the shooter"!

"So here we go again then"! the Inspector sighed through a mouthful of Danish. "Then we had better have a good look through his briefcase and see what we can turn up"!

"The employee files for the two missing survey team members are on top"! DC Wiseman was happy to report. "Obviously we cannot formerly identify the bodies solely on the basis of their photographs……….but as far as the photographs *are* concerned then at least we now know that these are definitely our bodies"!

"That is a good start; anything else in there"?

"A packet of supermarket sandwiches.........Waitrose, so not bought locally; a box of ten golf balls, two unopened packets of Marlboro reds and a bottle of something called Maker's Mark"!

"Only the best Bourbon that money can buy; and as the seal is not broken I do not think that this would be of much use to forensics.........nor the cigarettes for that matter"!

"We have already dusted it for fingerprints; those of the deceased were on there, but no others; I am guessing that the bottle was cleaned before it was put on the shelf which was probably the case if he shopped at Waitrose; and I would very much like to be around when you open *that* bad boy.......I love a drop of Bourbon"! the very shapely Dr Foxy pointed out.

"We should do that this evening; just as soon as the Super has gone home"!

"Oh.......does it have to be *this* evening Sir"! DC Wiseman grumbled.

"Of course………your hot date with the barmaid from the Midshipman. We shall save you some…………you have my word"!

"Save me some……..*my arse*"!

"I thought that you weren't overly keen on the spirits anyhow"?

"Anyway; how is *this* for a theory"? said the shapely Dr Foxy as she changed the subject a little. "Your man Greenslade comes down here to identify the bodies of his missing team members; but he is concerned about the proposed site so he stops off there to have a look around before meeting with you and Wiseman at the First and Last. Somebody knows that he is coming and they wait for him and murder him in Cosheston and then drive his body in his own car to the car park of the pub where they also know that the two of you will be"!

"But nobody outside of the Station knew that we were meeting with Mr Greenslade; my God Foxy………are you suggesting what I *think* you are suggesting; an inside job……a bent copper"!

"Well; it *is* a bit of a coincidence if you ask me"! Jane Foxy was convinced.

"But the decision over our lunchtime venue was a spur of the moment thing"! DC Wiseman pointed out. "It wasn't as if it was planned in advance or anything; we haven't been to that pub for weeks"!

The very shapely Dr Foxy took to scribbling on the Inspector's desk jotter.

Maybe your office is bagged? she wrote.

"Come again"? the Inspector wondered.

Dr Foxy examined her hastily scribbled note and she changed one of the letters.

Maybe your office is bugged?

"Holy shit"! and in a second the Inspector was scribbling on a spare desk jotter that he kept in his top drawer. *Car park……..right now; I am gasping for a smoke and they cannot possibly have bugged the entire car park.*

What if the bug has been placed about one or both of your persons Dr Foxy wrote down and she was correct in her spelling of everything this time.

We shall meet you there in five minutes the Inspector scribbled; and he and Wiseman got up and they left the room in silence and headed down the stairs.

-4-

Less than five minutes later the detectives joined the very shapely Dr Foxy in the Police Station's car park; dressed in nothing more than the little paper romper suits and booties as worn by the scenes of crime lot.

"Jane…………..I have been meaning to ask you this for a while; but how do you feel about cats"? the Inspector wondered as he lit his cigarette with a box of matches just in case his trusted Zippo had been bugged.

"Come again Inspector"?

"Well; we now find ourselves in a position where we don't know for sure who can be trusted.......apart from the immediate company.........if indeed there *is* any inside collusion; so the best thing that we could now from now on would be to carry on with the investigation as normal......but without any contact with the Station"!

"And where do the cats come into it again"?

"Well; our faces are known in Cosheston"! and the Inspector pointed to himself and DC Wiseman. "Mine is all too familiar because I live there; and Wiseman has been out to the pub a few times with me; but *your* face nobody knows.......and there is a small matter of a witches Coven that I should very much like infiltrated"!

"You are bloody joking.......aren't you"? but from the expression that was etched upon his face the very shapely Dr Foxy knew that the Inspector was *far* from joking.

"We shall go to my house to prepare first; the wife is away so we will not be disturbed and Wiseman and I need to get into some proper clothes before we catch our deaths"!

Chapter Seven

"This is ludicrous………I do not know the first thing about bloody witchcraft"! Dr Jane Foxy was still protesting.

"Aha……….I bet you know more than you actually think; but that much is immaterial. We have died your hair black so that you certainly *look* the part; the actual nitty-gritty of the witchcraft we shall Google"! and the Inspector explained the finer points of his plan. "We shall have you an expert in no time; and certainly before midnight and tonight's full moon"!

"And what would be happening tonight at midnight"?

"Maybe nothing; but I am guessing and hoping for a certain amount of frolicking in the moonlit countryside"!

"But I thought that the full moon was last night"! DC Wiseman was sure.

"Last night it was only *nearly* full; tonight is the full moon proper"!

"Would this frolicking happen to be *naked* frolicking"? Dr Foxy needed to know.

"You don't have to join in; you will be coming across them rather than joining forces with them straight away"!

"I am not having any tattoos"!

"Nor would I expect you to; I don't think that tattoos are at all compulsory in witchcraft circles"!

"So how on earth do I just *come across* a Coven of witches all frolicking around at midnight; surely they will be doing what they do somewhere well off the beaten track"! Dr Foxy was sure.

"Ah………and to that end young Wiseman has hatched a plan which I very much like the sound of"! and the Inspector nodded in Wiseman's direction.

"But I thought that you were out on your big date tonight"?

"I will cut it short; start making my excuses after the main course"! Wiseman reluctantly explained. "I should be with you by ten of the evening clock"!

"Look; I am a doctor of medicine and I was being bloody rhetorical; of course I know what dry bloody ice is. What I meant was what is it doing here……..in that refrigerated picnic hamper"! Dr Foxy explained herself when it came to her previous question.

"Well………we didn't want it to melt……or thaw……or liquefy; or whatever it is that dry ice does when it is exposed to the elements"! DC Wiseman pointed out now that he had returned from his hot date and they were once again huddled behind the trees of the far ridge at adjoined the paddock behind the old chapel.

"Do *either* of you understand the principle behind rhetoric"?

"Just picture this if you will; the witches of Westhaven are all as naked as and frolicking around and all of a sudden a bright light and a swirling mist appear at the edge of the wood"! and the Inspector held up his torch and he pointed it at the refrigerated picnic hamper. "Then *you* emerge from said mist………your hair all jet black and your borrowed robe of violent crimson rippling in the breeze; and you ask the naked lot from the village who has summoned you forth from the dark realm. The witches of Westhaven will actually *believe* that they have summoned up a dark force and they will be falling over each other to take you home with them and to make you part of their little occult family. You are in the club, so to speak; you are all miked up so that Wiseman and I will hear every word that you utter and we will never be far away if we are needed"!

"Do you really think that these people are daft enough to fall for it"?

"Trust me; I know them……….this plan of Wiseman's cannot possibly fail"!

"It is half past eleven Sir"! Wiseman informed his Inspector.

"Right then; places everybody………..they will surely start arriving soon"!

At eleven forty-five precisely the same four cars appeared as had appeared only the night before and they parked at the far end of the paddock; the lights in the old chapel flicked on once again and it wasn't long before the midnight revellers took to their frolicking and nakedness.

"Right; Wiseman………take the lid off the refrigerated picnic hamper and lets let the mist build up a bit before we start with the show"! the Inspector whispered.

"The lid is now off Sir"!

"Right then; lie on your back and get ready to shine your torch up through the mist and into the night sky. Have you got the red camera filter that I gave you"?

"In place Sir"!

The detectives took their positions on the ground and Dr Jane Foxy took her position in the middle of the trees and the dry ice fog.

"Ready Wiseman"?

"Ready Sir"!

"Right; three…..two..…one…..torches on"!

The sound of the frolicking and general naked merrymaking stopped almost instantly as Jane Foxy emerged from the red backlit mist; and in all fairness to DC Wiseman his visual effect worked tremendously well.

"Who has summoned me from the Dark Realm of eternal midnight"? Jane Foxy bellowed and the detectives had to turn down their earpieces or face being deafened.

The ring of stock still and suddenly very fearful witches all pushed their head witch to the front of their small gathering.

"I asked who of you summoned me"? Jane Foxy roared; and much louder than her previous bellowing if such a thing was possible.

"Um………me, I suppose"! and the detectives recognised the voice as belonging to Mrs Mills.

"And who might you be"? and Dr Foxy was still bellowing the fair bit.

"Um……..my secret name within the Coven is Granny Wrinkles; I am the leader of this Coven………along with my warlock husband Manbooba. And who might *you* be……….and where have you come from"?

"I am Maddalena……….Queen of the witches and bound concubine to the Phantom of the Unknown. Why have you summoned me to this place; are you having trouble with something and need my help………..us witches have to stick together"!

"Damn she's good"! the Inspector whispered.

"Ah………..we *might* need your help with a little something"! Granny mumbled.

"I was once mortal like you………..but now I wield great power in the Dark Realm of eternal midnight; but the one thing that the Dark Realm lacks is a really nice, fruity red wine"! Dr Foxy told them. "I will come with you to your Coven abode and drink a glass or two of wine"!

"Damn..........she is *very* good"! the Inspector whispered.

"As it happens my husband and I have just come back from a holiday in the Dordogne; we have *gallons* of red wine"! Granny Wrinkles admitted. "You would be honouring us with your presence"!

"Thank you; I would have preferred something a little more *New World*...........but I suppose that beggars cannot be choosers. Please lead the way...........but do me a favour and put some clothes on first"!

"Shit..........what do we do now"? DC Wiseman wondered as the witches of Westhaven all pulled their robes back on and they climbed back into their cars.

"We'll just run down through the woods and back to my place.........that way cuts off quite a large corner; and then we can jump into your car. Then it's back to the village and the Westhaven estate. We will lose radio contact with Dr Foxy for ten minutes or so; but that will prove no great hardship considering that we know where they are taking her"!

"The cars are leaving the car park Sir"!

"Then we should start with the cross country running"!

The detectives were just pulling into the Westhaven estate when the Inspector's radio started getting all crackly and Dr Foxy could be heard speaking again as the transmitter obviously came back into range.

"I am quite sure that I did say something about not being able to get hold of a nice and fruity *red* in the Dark Realm; and here I am presented with a glass of something white that is also very sweet"! and Maddalena did complain somewhat.

"But as white wines go you *have* to admit that it is a very lovely white wine"! Granny Wrinkles replied as she topped up the glass of the Witch Queen.

"Admittedly it is very nice; but sweet wines tend to give me a bit of a head"!

"Try this then" and Manbooba intervened. "This is a very exquisite Pecharmant red from Bergerac"! and Manbooba offered her a glass of red.

"Bergerac……….wasn't he that copper on Jersey or Guernsey or somewhere like that"? Maddalena wondered with a slight slur that she hoped nobody else noticed.

"Oh………so you have TV in the Dark Realm then"? Manbooba wondered.

"Like I said…………..I too was once mortal; now this red wine is *seriously* the dog's bollocks"!

"I hope she doesn't get hopelessly drunk and end up blowing it"! the Inspector hoped out loud.

"Now then; and down to business; what was it that you wanted my help with"? and Maddalena put her very efficient business head back on.

"Well………you see………it's like this.." Granny began but Manbooba cut her off mid-sentence.

"If I could just say……….why don't we leave this until tomorrow morning when we are all feeling fresh and rested; tomorrow is flexi-time Wednesday so Granny and I won't have to worry about leaving early for work"!

"I should really be getting back to the Dark Realm; the Phantom of the Unknown will be wondering where on earth I have got to"!

"Nonsense; stay for just one night and let us show you some *proper* hospitality; I do not know what the catering facilities are like in the Dark Realm but I have the makings of a wonderful fry-up for when morning comes"! Manbooba told her with a wink.

"Oh yes……….please say you'll stay; you could teach us some of your magic………if you were of a mind to"! Granny Wrinkles also implored of her.

"Very well; I shall stay for one night……….provided that you unleash another bottle of the Bergerac"!

"And *that* probably means that we will be sleeping here in this bloody car for the night"! DC Wiseman realised.

"It certainly looks that way at the minute. How would you feel about skulking around in the bushes for a while just in case Dr Foxy needs us; I can nip home and get some blankets and pillows"!

"And maybe a bottle of something to help us pass the very cold and wee hours of the morning"?

"As long as you like the Barbadian rum; we drank most of everything else the other night and I have left the Maker's Mark in my office draw"!

"Mount Gay or Cockspur"?

"Aha………….a rum connoisseur"!

-4-

The Inspector was rudely awoken by an urgent rapping upon the rear passenger window of Wiseman's pool car.

"We have got to get out of here…………and we should go about it very quickly. Now open the bloody door"!

"Dr Foxy…………what is wrong…………have we been rumbled"? the Inspector wondered as he was startled from his dreaming.

"Granny Wrinkles and Manbooba are presently in their kitchen rustling up a full-on fried breakfast………both as naked as the days upon which they were born; and hash browns and man-knockers are *not* my idea of a fry-up; especially as I have had a shower and all of the black shit has washed out of my hair. I left them a note saying that I had been summoned back to the Dark Realm on some business or other and that I would be back to see them on the next full moon"!

"Damn it; I had hoped that we would be able to retrieve much more in the way of intelligence from them before you would have to leave"! the Inspector cursed.

"I did recover a fair bit of intelligence from them last night after I turned in"! Dr Foxy revealed. "I could hear them talking when they were in bed……….painfully thin walls in that house so I am glad that all they were doing was talking; but their conversation was probably too muted for the wire to pick up"!

By this time the Inspector was back behind the wheel and Dr Foxy was climbing onto the rear seat.

"Let's go and get a coffee; I will tell you all about it"!

"We shall go to my house; I need to have a bit of a tidy up before my wife and son return home from Devon later on this afternoon; and we can grab the bicycles on the way"!

"You have got to be joking"! and the Inspector was fairly reduced to fits of the hysterics in his very own kitchen.

"I kid thee not"!

"Wife swappers………..as in *swingers*"? DC Wiseman also had to double check just in case he had misheard the very shapely Dr Foxy. "Up in Woodfield Grove"?

"A whole street just *full* of them; Granny Wrinkles believes them to be behind the murders; and before you ask there is absolutely *no* way that I am going to try and infiltrate *their* sordid little group"!

"But why would a bunch of swingers want to murder two German technicians from a solar panel survey team"?

"You tell me; *you* are the copper"!

"Curiouser and curiouser"! DC Wiseman sniggered.

"Right then; there is a young WPC that I know of who has recently moved to the bottom of Woodfield Grove with her husband and two small children; they would *certainly* not be a party to such carrying on…………..but they have probably been living there long enough to be aware of the rumours"! the Inspector was hopeful. "We can't go back to the Station; that much is out…………we should go to see the WPC and see what shift she is on; if she is not there then her husband will be because of the children"!

"And you are sure that they are not the swinging type"? DC Wiseman asked with a mischievous smile.

"Definitely not; they are both of them of the chapel persuasion. Come along then; this house is surely now tidy enough to pass the wife's inspection and the bicycles are back in the shed; we should away to Woodfield Grove"!

The detectives and Dr Foxy were invited into the house that sat at the very bottom of Woodfield Grove. It transpired that WPC Palmer had just started a week off and her husband had already taken the children to school before taking himself off to work.

"The Super is a bit concerned that you haven't been into the office for a while.........as are the caterers in the mobile unit; everybody's talking about you"! WPC Palmer told them as they waited for the kettle to boil. "The Super can't figure out how to work your coffee machine and the new interactive murder board thing seems to be on the blink"!

"Sarah..........what are your neighbours like"?

"My neighbours...........well, if you put fifty kids with downs syndrome in the same room there's *going* to be a lot of hugging"!

"Come again"? wondered DC Wiseman.

"Well; they're a bit of a cliquey bunch.......and rather too familiar"! Sarah explained herself. "Everybody up there seems to be always in and out of one another's houses. Matt swears blind that there are being keys chucked into a bowl; but that's more than likely him being a little overly cynical"!

"Let is just say, and quite hypothetically, that if there *were* keys being thrown into a bowl then in which house would the *main* bowl most likely be"? the Inspector wondered.

"My God; are you telling me they really *are* swingers; oh my God..............is this anything to do with the murder investigation"?

"Let's just say that it might well be an avenue worth investigating"! the Inspector admitted.

"Number thirteen.........the bungalow on the left as you go up; start off with number thirteen; now.........milk or cream in your coffee"?

Number thirteen was a bungalow not at all dissimilar to the other bungalows in an estate made up mostly of houses; save for the fact the front garden remained a front garden rather than a huge slab of concrete upon which cars and small vans could be parked; a small front garden but a very pretty affair with gold coloured pebbles and plants in all manner of pots and a notice which pleaded with the local dogs not todo their pooing amongst the pretty pebbles.

The Inspector rang at the doorbell; with no reply. And then he knocked upon the angel-reclining door knocker; still no reply; and after a few heavy CID style knockings upon the front door the Inspector realised that the front door was actually off its latch and so he pushed the door inward.

The carpet inside the doorway was red and patterned and looked as though it would have been equally at home in an Indian Restaurant. The only item of furniture within that hallway was a crescent shaped table upon which stood a telephone and a dog-eared telephone directory; and the edges of the red and patterned carpet were thick with the same coloured sand that the Inspector had dropped all over the briefing room floor only a short while previous.

"I know; I can see it as well"! the Inspector told an excited DC Wiseman as he pointed at all of the sand.

"Is this where it came from Sir"? the Detective Constable wondered. "Have you been throwing your *own* keys into a bowl in this house"?

"I have never been up this street before……..or into this house, for that matter"! the Inspector was sure. "Well……..apart from walking up here a few times to get to the football pitch………but that was years ago…..before I was married even"!

The detectives and Dr Foxy walked the length of the hall and they entered the kitchen at the very end of it; or at least they entered the space at the end of the hall that they naturally assumed the kitchen would be occupying.

The kitchen space was an open tract of desert that looked out upon some sand dunes; and when they turned to look at the hallway from whence they had only recently walked they found that the hallway had disappeared and all around them was sand and very little in the way of anything else.

DC Wiseman had the bright idea of quickly walking back the way that they had come before he lost his bearings; hoping that the hallway and the crescent shaped telephone table would magically reappear………..but he had no such luck. They were now standing in the middle of a desert and all around them was sand; nothing else………..just sand.

"What the bloody hell do you suppose *this* is all about"? DC Wiseman just had to ask.

"Gentlemen………and lady; welcome to the desert of the real"! said the voice that suddenly appeared as if from nowhere.

"That is a line from The Matrix"! DC Wiseman was sure.

"That it might well be; but I am not Morpheus and this is not some training program"! said one of the two persons that approached them. The figures were dressed from head to toe in billowing robes of blue and gold; and as they drew nearer the mysterious figures removed the veils from their heads that served to keep the sand away from their faces.

"Bloody hell; Rick Dylan………and his best friend Bruno"! said an incredulous Inspector. "So it was *you* that clocked me over the back of the head the other day and brought me to this place"!

"Actually that was all Bruno's doing; but we work as one"!

"What on earth is going on?"

"The end of the world as we know it; unless we act very quickly"!

Chapter Eight

"Where are we"?

"Physically and spatially you are still in the kitchen to number thirteen, Woodfield Grove"! Rick explained.

"But it looks somewhat different to what it did a few minutes ago"! the Inspector said with a confused face.

"Number thirteen is the portal"!

"Portal to where"?

"To here"!

"I am seriously going to nick you for wasting Police time"!

"Look; you have obviously heard the rumours for yourself otherwise you would not be standing here right now; everybody in the village who does not live up this street assumes that the residents of Woodfield Grove are wife-swappers because they are always in and out of one another's houses; but in actual fact they are actually only in and out of number thirteen because number thirteen is the gateway"! and Bruno had a go at explaining things.

"But gateway to *where*……..and do not say *here* because then I will get upset and you will be mentioning Police brutality and complaining that the handcuffs are cutting into your wrists"!

"The gateway to a parallel dimension……..or at least that what we *think* this is; we are still on earth………just not an earth that we are familiar with"!

"So how do we get back; number thirteen seems to have pretty much disappeared"! and Wiseman pointed to where he thought the kitchen used to be.

"Ah………..we haven't figured that much out as of yet"! Bruno was honest. "We have tried retracing our steps but that much hasn't worked; and the toing and froing of the Woodfield Grover's seems to have ceased for a while; but we are confident that if there is a gateway *in* then there should also be a gateway *out*………nature always finding a balance and everything"!

"What"? and the Inspector was quite incredulous.

"We have been here pretty much since the incident in the Police car park"! Rick told them.

"Have you tried clicking your heels together three times and saying *there's no place like home* over and over"? Dr Foxy wondered.

"Yeah; done that………..and we have also tried *computer; end simulation………holodeck off* and various combinations of *make it so* and *engage*"!

"No joy then"?

"Obviously not"!

"So just who or what are the residents of Woodfield Grove; are they aliens or something"? and the Inspector was having difficulty getting his head around the whole dimension jumping principle.

"Not at all; they are human just like us; the only difference is they have mastered the art of jumping between parallel dimensions"!

"That is just make-believe stuff for the movies"! Wiseman was sure.

"And yet here you are; and they said the same thing about time travel"! Rick pointed out.

"But time travel *is* impossible"! Wiseman was also sure.

"*Actually* Theo, time travel *is* possible; Rick and Bruno here are *masters* of it………..although that much is to remain a very well-kept secret if ever we are to get out of here"!

"You kept *that* quiet Sir"!

"The less you know the less I would ask you to lie"!

"So how the bloody hell *do* we get out of here"? Wiseman had to ask.

"Search us"! Rick told him.

"All right then; if we *have* just walked through an inter-dimensional portal thing then all we have to do is sit tight and wait for some of the residents of Woodfield Grove to come through on whatever business it is that they are up to…..and then we can follow them back"! the Inspector was sure. "If they are in and out as much as it is rumoured in the village then it will surely not be very long before one or two of them show up"!

"All aboard"! said the voice that was very new to the conversation; and a head suddenly appeared over the nearest sand dune.

"Who or *what* the bloody hell is *that*"? and the Inspector pointed as he wondered.

"That man is an enigma all of his very own making"! Rick said as he waved cheerfully. "His hat says *gatekeeper*; his lapel badge says *conductor*; all *we* know is………..he is called The Bluns"!

"The Bluns"?

"The Bluns; what with his surname being Blunsden and everything; we know that he is one of us………in so much as he is from our own dimension because Bruno and I can both remember him being our postman when we were little"! Rick did his best to explain. "It was rumoured that he emigrated to Australia; but once again we think that that is village tittle-tattle that has gone somewhat awry; but we *do* think that he has been stuck in this dimension for so long that he has gone stark staring tonto and he thinks that he is a conductor upon an imaginary train"!

"All aboard"! The Bluns repeated. "I am afraid that all the seats are taken; but there is standing room in the refreshments carriage and we have many cans of McEwan's that have only just passed their sell-by dates"! The Bluns continued; and then he blew upon a small and silver coloured whistle and he waved a little flag. "All aboard then……….are you lot deaf or what"?

"So there is no train then"? the Inspector assumed.

"Probably not"! Rick seemed convinced.

"So you haven't actually gone and had a look or anything"?

"Well, no………..not really; he keeps saying that this train of his is just on the other side of that sand dune just over there; but Bruno and I have both been rather reluctant to leave this spot just in case we miss somebody coming or going through the gateway and then not being able to find our way back because this sandy landscape is all rather monotonous; and then there is the fact that The Bluns is stone cold bonkers"!

"Right; stay here for now; I shall go and investigate"! the Inspector told them and he set out across the sand toward The Bluns and the nearest sand dune.

When the Inspector and The Bluns reached the top of the dune the Inspector turned to the others and he called out to them; waving furiously at the same time.

"You had *all* better come up here and take a look at this"! the Inspector shouted through cupped hands; and so they all did just that.

-2-

Ten feet below their feet, but some twenty feet away as the dune lay, a silver bullet-shaped train sat at a station. The station appeared to be a small and rural single platform affair that they were all quite familiar with; and said station was sandwiched between two tunnels that disappeared into the sand; and the silver bullet-shaped train hummed almost silently at the platform as they all stood there and looked on in a state of some bewilderment.

"Isn't she a beauty"? The Bluns asked rhetorically.

"A train"? said Wiseman.

"Why do you think I was shouting *all aboard*"?

"But a train………in the middle of a strange desert"? Wiseman expanded.

"It is much more comfortable than a camel"!

"So where does this train go"? the Inspector wondered as he started down the dune in the direction of the station and everybody else took to following him.

"Well………this way or that way"! and The Bluns pointed at each of the tunnels.

"Right; at the *moment* I shall not yet read you the riot act about the wasting of Police time; so………and thinking a little more carefully about your answer this time, where does the train go when it leaves the station"?

"To the *next* station, presumably; I don't know for sure; I have never before ridden upon it"!

"But you seem very keen for us to get on it………what with all of your *all-a-boarding*"! the Inspector was quick to remind The Bluns.

"Ah………well………I have known of the existence of this train for quite some time; but I have never yet rustled up the courage to climb aboard………what with me being here on my own some; but if *you lot* get on then I promise that I will get on with you"! The Bluns promised.

"Is there a *proper* conductor or any other such staff around here"?

"I don't think so; you see, when I first came across this train something happened to me that caused me to pass out; and when I awoke I had upon my back this strange jacket which came with its own lapel badge……….and also this strange hat"! and The Bluns pointed at them both. "I think that *I* actually might be the conductor"!

"Well……..if that is the case then I should like to go *that* way"! and the Inspector pointed in the direction that would have been south in their own dimension. "This dimension's equivalent of Pembroke might well lie in that direction……..and it would only be a small hop away"!

"Right…………all aboard then"! and The Bluns shepherded them toward the bullet-shaped train.

"After you"! the Inspector insisted.

"Come again"? The Bluns wondered.

"I would like it if *you* were to get on the train first; and then the rest of us will follow"!

"So………..the bit about all of the seats upon the train being taken was obviously just a bit of a fabrication"! DC Wiseman observed as they stood in the two empty carriages that were the extent of the train. "What about the bit when it came to the buffet car and the cans of McEwan's; I don't really care what it is but I could really do with a drink right about now"!

"Ah………….maybe just a bit of poetic licence"? The Bluns suggested. "I might well have stretched the truth there a little bit just to get you interested"! he admitted.

"So………….no beer then"!

"None that I have seen whilst peering in through the windows from the outside; but who knows……..there might well be some somewhere; it's probably just a question of finding it"!

"So………..if you are the train's *conductor*……..then where would be the train's *driver*"? the Inspector wondered.

"To be brutally honest with you I have never seen anyone else anywhere near this train; and I am thinking that the driving of a train such as this is probably a straightforward task that is probably also entrusted to the train's conductor"! and The Bluns explained his theory. "Now; there is a cab at either end of this train; if I have a wander down the carriage that is at the end of the train that is pointing in the direction that we would like to travel and then start pressing at some buttons then maybe that might do it"?

"If it is all the same with you then I will have young DC Wiseman here pressing at the buttons; he has a natural technical leaning when it comes to the pressing of buttons"! the Inspector was sure. "Right; everybody else sit down and strap yourselves in and get ready for goodness knows bloody what"!

Nothing particularly Earth shattering happened, irrespective of what dimension you happened to be in; and nothing even remotely terrifying either. All that happened was for the doors to swish very quietly closed; and with a small initial shudder the train started to move in the direction that they all hoped that it would; and not at all fast either.

"I have come across a series of levers which I think will make the train go faster"! DC Wiseman shouted back along the carriage.

"You just make sure that you know where the brakes are and how they work before you think about setting any land speed records"! the Inspector advised him.

DC Wiseman pressed at a few more switches and buttons until the train's headlights came on; and after switching off the piped music he happily left The Bluns at the controls.

"I can see a little bit of daylight at the end of the tunnel; but at the moment it is little more than a tiny pinprick………it looks like being a few miles away and these tunnels must be *very* straight"! DC Wiseman was happy to report. "I don't suppose that anybody found that beer that The Bluns was on about, did they"?

"There is nothing"! Bruno was very *unhappy* to report.

-4-

The train blasted out of the tunnel and into the sunlight and the glass of the carriage windows tinted automatically before anybody in their party was blinded by the sudden and harsh contrast. The Bluns brought the train to a stop at a much larger station and all disembarked and took to standing on the platform.

"Which way do you think Sir"?

"That way"! and the Inspector pointed.

"You seem very sure Sir"!

"Well; just look over there, Wiseman………there is a footbridge that would take us over the railway lines and onto what looks to be the main platform on the other side. That suggests to me then that that is the direction that we should be taking; just up to the top of that sand dune over there and then we shall see what we shall see"!

"I wonder if this dimension has anything in the way of public houses"? Bruno was first to wonder out loud.

They used the footbridge and they crossed the railway line and they set off at quite a brisk pace and the towering top of the nearest sand dune was very quickly reached.

"Well bloody hell…………*the sea*"! DC Wiseman gawped. "I wasn't expecting to see a lovely blue sea in a land so full of sand and little else"!

"The sea indeed; and Wiseman……..you should look more closely; the curve of the bay…………that huge rock just there;

this is indeed Tenby"! the Inspector was sure. "Or at least this dimension's equivalent of the Tenby that we all know"!

"And look down there……….close to the water's edge"! and Dr Foxy pointed. "Houses……….lots of houses"!

"And where there are houses it is probably safe to assume that there will be *public houses*"! Bruno was sure. "Last one down there gets them in"!

"Not so fast Bruno"! and the Inspector pulled the almost fleeing late-teenager back by the scruff of his neck. "It would probably be wise just to *observe* the place for a while; pull up a dune and have a seat………..and once again we shall see what we shall see"!

"I spy with my little eye……….something beginning with S"! Bruno broke the silence a little while later.

"Right…………well it's either sand, sea, sun or sky"! Rick was reasonably sure.

"All right then; something beginning with D"!

"Dune"! said Dr Foxy.

"Do you think that it might be safe to go and have a look at those houses now Inspector"? Rick suggested. "We have observed for a goodly while now and there have been none of the comings or goings; the place looks as deserted as"!

"I have just been thinking exactly the same thing; but just to err on the side of caution I think that we should head down the ridge to our left so that we can then approach the houses from the east rather than just heading down slap-bang in the middle of them"! was the way the Inspector was thinking. "Who knows what will be waiting for us down there"?

"Do you know..........but it feels to me that we are walking on a road; well.........more like it feels as though there is a road underneath all of this sand"! Bruno was sure a short time later when they had reached the bottom of the sand dune and they had turned to walk toward the houses.

"In the Tenby that *we* know this would be the road that overlooks the North Beach and the harbour; just up there would be the ruin that was once the Gatehouse"! the Inspector told them in his guise as tour guide.

"Then *that* surely means that up the hill and just around the corner would be the Sun Inn *and* The Lamb; *one* of them might exist in this dimension"! Bruno was hopeful.

"I wonder what used to exist to our right before the desert took over"? Dr Foxy wondered.

"How are you so sure that *anything* previously existed there"?

"Because Bruno is quite right"! Dr Foxy answered Rick's question. "Beneath the sand beneath our feet there is a road; we know this because of the relative ease of our walking.........but over a period, and goodness knows how long, the sand has encroached right over it. This place might once have been identical to the Tenby that we all know........and then the sand somehow took over"!

"If that *is* the case then I wonder what the hell happened here"?

"Here we are then………..the Sun Inn"! and Bruno brought the expedition to a halt.

"The windows are all boarded up………..just like the Sun Inn that *we* are familiar with"! and it was Rick's turn to point out the obvious.

"That they are………..but the front door is open and all we can do is but try"! Bruno was resolute.

"Hold it right there"! and once again Inspector Gallant had to manhandle Bruno by the scruff of his neck. "Look down there……..in the sand………footprints, if I am not very much mistaken"!

"They seem fairly recent as well"! Dr Foxy said after a cursory examination.

"Footprints leading into a pub are not that out of the ordinary; it was probably their most recent customer"! Bruno was convinced.

"For the love of God, Bruno; just take a look around. What is left of this place is a ghost town in the middle of a barren wasteland; there simply *are* no customers"! and the Inspector sounded fairly confident of as much.

"Good; if that is the case then we shall not have to wait too long at the bar"! and Bruno wriggled out of the Inspector's grasp and into the pub.

The interior of the Sun Inn was empty except for the usual bar furniture and all of the sand that had blown in through the open front door. They followed the Inspector who followed the footprints to where they snaked behind the bar; and then they all stopped at the wall where the footprints suddenly and mysteriously stopped. Bruno fiddled with the taps on the bar's many pumps to see if there was any beer to be had……..but there was not so much as a drip; and further examination showed that there was not even so much as a part bottle of anything behind that bar.

"Um………there are some out of date pork scratchings over here"! Jane Foxy noticed.

"Ah; that is a tradition as common as a turkey or a goose at Christmas; unfortunately it would be impossible to fathom out from the pork scratchings just how long this place has been in the state it is in because we have no way of knowing just how out of date the pork scratchings were in the first place"! Rick explained. "We could be out by months………or more likely *years*"!

"Right then; this place must surely have a cellar"! Bruno was sure after only a moment of not saying much. "There might be *all* sorts in the cellar; bottled beer, wine, crisps……..the list could well go on and on"!

"Does anyone else think that it is rather unusual that the footprints in the sand stop just here"? the Inspector wondered aloud and he pressed at the only button that was on the wall just in front of them.

There followed a humming sound in the middle distance just like a lift motor might make; and then the humming stopped as something clanked and clunked behind the wall that was right in front of them. The wall that was just in front of them came alive with blue flashes of static electricity for a moment; and then the wall turned into a set of lift doors that swished almost silently open and they all regarded the inside of the lift that suddenly appeared.

"A lift"? said Wiseman.

"No shit"! said the Inspector.

"All aboard"! said The Bluns.

"Um………assuming that the G button is for *this* floor there appears to be only one other button; and the arrow on this illuminated button is pointing down"! Dr Foxy revealed.

"Right; I think that it might be a good idea if some of us where to stay up here while the others investigate down below; there is no telling *what* might be waiting for us down there; it might spell certain death"! the Inspector worried.

"I know where you are coming from………but I think that we should stick together; safety in numbers and all that"! and it was Dr Foxy that voiced her opinion. "And at the bottom of that lift there might well be a way of getting back to our own dimension……….and I am all for going home"!

"Dr Foxy is right"! Rick agreed. "I for one am not for staying up here; the bar is as dry as and this place fairly gives me the creeps; and you lot have not yet experienced a night in this horrible desert world; Bruno and I have and we are all for getting in the lift"!

"Amen"! said Bruno.

"All aboard"! The Bluns reiterated.

The lift doors went *ping* and they swished almost silently open once again.

"End of the line"! said The Bluns. "WOTCHA COOKIE"! The Bluns then shouted.

"What"? wondered the Inspector; as did everybody else.

"Cookie………..he is my mate"! The Bluns explained. "He's down here somewhere; he's *always* down here somewhere"!

"So where is he then; and while we are on the subject where precisely *is* here"? the Inspector wondered.

The Bluns stepped out of the lift; and in the darkness he fumbled around on the wall that was nearest to the lift door until he found the switch that he was looking for; and he cleared his throat before he turned the switch in a clockwise manner.

A bank of overhead lights clunked and then flashed on and illuminated their new surroundings.

"Cookie is down here somewhere; mark my words"! and The Bluns seemed to be at his most lucid; at least since they had met him.

The chamber in which they were now standing was almost perfectly round and had obviously been hewn from solid rock somewhere along the line. A walkway existed from the lift that hugged the wall of the chamber all of the way around; and in the middle of the chamber behind a built-up bun wall was a huge reservoir that was quite full to its brim.

"Not much in the way of the drinking water up top.......you might have noticed"! The Bluns said to everyone as they stared with open mouths. "But the artesian wells of old still exist; and this here is one of them"!

Dr Foxy took to examining the sides of the well at the point where they were presently standing……..a manmade wall built up to about three feet in height ringed the reservoir all the way around; and although it was probably not tall enough to prevent anyone falling in it seemed to be doing a pretty good job of stopping the water from falling out.

"Inspector; remember the two drowned bodies that started this whole investigation and I told you how there was bruising on their torsos consistent with being forcibly bent over something when they drowned; well……………I think that we have found that something and the very place where they were done for"!

"This is getting harder and harder to believe; so…….the two Germans were murdered down here; their bodies then dragged to the lift and then across the dunes to be taken away on the train; only to be dragged through the gateway thing and then dumped in the village in a very poor attempt to make their deaths look like suicide; the question that remains is why"?

"They must have stumbled across the gateway thing when they were going about their solar panel surveying business; and they maybe saw too much"? and it was DC Wiseman's turn to muse about the situation.

"But the proposed solar park is at entirely the other end of the village from Woodfield Grove"! the Inspector thought it pertinent to point out.

"All right then; how about the German pair were a couple of some sort who heard on the often faulty village grapevine that Woodfield Grove was a street full of the swingers and they wanted to get in on the rumpy-pumpy action"! Dr Foxy suggested.

"*That* little scenario is *much* more likely; so………they go to the Grove looking for a little of the after-survey nookie; they walk into number thirteen because they have heard on the often faulty grapevine that that is where the majority of the key-throwing takes place; and then they stumble upon the gateway thing to the parallel dimension. They are done for so that the secret remains just that………a secret. But why go to all the trouble of taking their bodies back through the gateway thing to Cosh. In trying to keep things a secret the murderers have unwittingly achieved the exact opposite"!

"They can't bury anybody down here"! said the voice that was strange to most of them.

"Wotcha Cookie"! said The Bluns once again. "No.......he is all right"! The Bluns told the Inspector as the detective started with his squaring up to the newcomer. "This is my friend Cookie that I have been telling you about"!

"We gathered as much"! Dr Foxy spoke for all of them.

"Could you imagine the smell in a town under the ground if they started burying their dead"? Cookie wondered rhetorically. "They normally just take them up in the lift and dump them in the tide at high water"!

"And yet the bodies of the two Germans were taken all the way to Cosh and dumped in a manner that could only arouse more suspicion; I still say that this is symbolic of something"! the Inspector was sure. "Cookie.........you spoke of an underground town; what is this place..........is it your home"!

"It is *now*; but I am actually a Monkton boy; from the Monkton that *you* are all familiar with"! Cookie began to explain. "I came across this place about a year ago; the missus had just left me and taken the kids with her……..I had nothing to go back for, so I stayed. You see, my painting and decorating skills were in very high demand because of them just having created this new and underground town; and there is no currency so I had to be paid in kind……..and there are *lots* of pretty women down here"! and Cookie winked. "And on the subject of which, who would be this lovely lady in your party………with the really amazing baps"?

"I am Dr Jane Foxy; and if you so much as *breathe* on my baps I'll smash your face in"!

"Oh yes…………I like 'em with a bit of fire"! Cookie said with another wink and he extended his hands for a bit of a grope; but before he could get his hands anywhere near that bosom Dr Foxy unleashed a right hook that caught Cookie squarely underneath his chin; sending him sprawling backwards over the bun wall that surrounded the reservoir and into its deep, black and all-consuming waters.

"Ah………..I would suggest that *now* would be the time to run away and find somewhere to hide"! The Bluns suggested and his face looked serious. "The interior walls of that artesian well are flat smooth and it's very, *very* deep; poor Cookie is almost certainly a goner..............but if by some chance he isn't then he is surely big and ugly enough to take care of himself"! The Bluns was sure. "For the time being, and in the not too distant future I would say that we have troubles enough of our own"! and as The Bluns was hypothesising an alarm that was really quite painful to the ears of the listener started with its shrill caterwauling.

"Back to the lift"! the Inspector was sure.

"No; there isn't time for that; we should go *this* way"! and they all scampered after The Bluns who led them around the corner in the opposite direction to the lift and down a short flight of hand carved steps.

They had just managed to conceal themselves in the shadows either side of a large doorway when the same doorway veritably burst open and a swarm of large people dressed from head to toe entirely in black erupted forth and ran up the hand carved stone steps.

"They are some sort of guard"! The Bluns whispered to the Inspector who was crushed up against him now that the double doors had been flung wide open. "I think that they wear the full face leather masks just in case they are sent up in the lift; it was quite calm when we were out there, but there are times when the sand can get some wind behind it and it really chafes"!

"We can't stay here for long; they will surely spot us when they come back this way"!

"When they have all passed us by we will nip within and acquire us some of the head-to-toe black uniforms; we will then be able to mingle amongst them and nobody will be any the wiser; I have done it before on a few occasions and have never been discovered"!

"Have they got any guns"? Wiseman wondered. "I would probably feel an awful lot better if there were a few guns between us"!

"More weapons than you can shake a stick at"! The Bluns promised.

Chapter Nine

"What"? wondered DC Wiseman.

"Your choice of weapons"! and The Bluns pointed at the arsenal as they pulled on their leather face masks.

"But you said more *guns* than you could shake a stick at"! and DC Wiseman sounded somewhat disparaging with his pointing out.

"I did no such thing; what I said was more *weapons* than you could shake a stick at"! The Bluns pointed out back.

"But these are just *sticks*"!

"This is what they use; and they are fashioned from the wood of an ash tree and as such are really whippy; *I* wouldn't like to be on the receiving end of one of them; I bet they come *really* tight"!

"I quite like the feel of them"! said Dr Foxy as she brandished hers like it was a broadsword.

"So………..are you an Obi Wan Kenobi or a Darth Vader sort of a girl"? The Bluns wondered.

"More of an Anakin Skywalker before he turned to the dark side"! Dr Foxy was sure.

"We should get out to the aquifer and start mingling with the guards before they are stood down"! the Inspector was sure.

"What was the alarm for anyhow"? DC Wiseman wondered as he selected the longest stick of ash that was available to him.

"Foreign body in the drinking water is the most likely reason; they are quite mad for their clean drinking water down here…….which you can understand"! The Bluns speculated. "Now then; we have all bagged the spare guards' uniforms with the yellow shoulder patches; this means that we are quite high ranking and we should be able to wander anywhere that we wish; and we should probably go now"!

"Look……….mine was a simple mistake with no malice intended"! The Bluns protested. "I felt sure that a yellow flash upon one's shoulders displayed a high rank within the guard"!

"And yet here we are in the frighteningly deep water of the aquifer under orders to retrieve the body"! DC Wiseman said what everybody already knew as they treaded water. "I do not think that the guards with the yellow flashes upon their shoulders are particularly high ranking. They will probably have us cleaning out toilets next"!

"Well……at least the rest of the guard have left us to our own devices and are not standing over us"! and it was Dr Foxy that looked on the bright side. "We can have a little swim around for a while; report back that the intruder made it out of the water and as far as the lift and has run away……..and nobody will be any the wiser"!

"Until somebody wants their bloody ceiling painted"! the Inspector reminded her. "*Then* they might start putting two and two together"!

"Come off it………..they must have somebody else down here who is good with a roller; it is not exactly a rocket science now, is it"?

The Bluns coughed and spluttered and he returned to the surface of the water a few moments later.

"I have had a good look around down there; and there is no sign of a body *anywhere*"! he was sure. "I reckon that he *has* got out without us noticing"!

"Then we must be on our guard just in case he decided to blow the whistle on us or something"! the Inspector advised everybody. "But as far as we know this Cookie fella doesn't know that we have acquired the uniform of the guard; we still have the element of surprise on our side"!

"And at least the water isn't at all cold"! DC Wiseman was grateful as he floated around on his back. "I mean………it's not exactly *Turkish bath hot*; but it is not at all unpleasant"!

They swam to the side of the reservoir and they heaved themselves out and onto the path using the ropes that had been left there for them.

"So………what is the story when it comes to your friend Cookie, anyhow"? the Inspector couldn't help but wonder after meeting him only the once. "Is he or was he playing with a full deck"?

"Well; he's basically all there and he is a good bloke; but there was an unfortunate tequila based incident a while back and he has never quite been the same after that"!

"Aha………the demon drink strikes again; and I should say that the drinking of tequila needs some management and self-discipline"!

"Don't judge him too harshly; it wasn't strictly speaking the *drinking* of tequila that did for him"!

"So what happened"? the Inspector wondered as they all heaved themselves out of the reservoir and they rested upon the path as they caught their various breaths.

"Well………..it was a Saturday and Cookie and his wife had been invited to a wedding reception. It was at this wedding reception that Cookie noticed some youngsters doing the whole tequila drinking thing…….with the limes and the salt and everything. Cookie walked over and he stopped the kids doing what they were doing and he told them that *he* would show them how to drink tequila properly"!

"So what happened"?

"Well; he picked up a whole lime and he ate it like it was an apple; then he downed half a bottle of tequila; and then he poured the contents of the salt cellar onto the bar………and he snorted it"!

"Oh man………..that *must* have hurt"! DC Wiseman was sure.

"Rumours abounded on the night that he had cut his own foot off with a steak knife to take his mind off the pain when he was waiting for the ambulance to turn up…………but I think that that was just the alcohol exaggerations because I have since seen both of his feet and they were both definitely attached to the ends of his legs. But he did eventually go very red of the face and pass out; and he stayed passed out for the best part of two weeks. When he finally awoke he discovered that his business had gone to the wall; his wife had taken the kids and had gone to Australia with an estate agent called Gregory; and after all that Cookie became a bit of a recluse"!

"I wonder what long term damage the snorting of salt would do to your septum"? DC Wiseman wondered.

"I think that his septum is or was the least of his worries"! The Bluns seemed sure. "Right then; what do you think we should do now"?

"I have been giving that some thought"! the Inspector admitted. "Now; apart from the guards who all went back to their barracks or whatever else they call it, everybody else walked along that path"! and the Inspector pointed the path out; not that there was another path to choose from. "I should very much like to see where that path leads"!

They had to walk through rather an ornate archway to get to the path that the Inspector had pointed out; but once through the archway the tunnel in which they now found themselves kept the shape of the arch for as far as the eye could see. The tunnel was just tall enough to walk without any of them having to bend their backs; and the tunnel was well lit and tended to and there was even a handrail fashioned from rope upon either side.

After a few minutes of walking in silence they emerged in a large cavern that took all of their various breaths away.

"Well good bloody God..........who would have expected anything like this"? wondered DC Wiseman who was the first to start with his breathing again.

They found themselves standing upon a gantry at the very top of this new cavern. The ceiling had been painted sky blue with occasional white cotton-wool clouds; and down below them, at the bottom of a flight of metal steps, was an exact representation of the Tudor Square in the Tenby that they all knew. Each building had its own brightly painted façade; and each was even more meticulously maintained than they had ever noticed when standing in the *other* Tudor Square.

"Do you suppose that either Tenby House or The Lifeboat Tavern are public houses in *this* domain"? Bruno wondered and he used both hands to point at either side of the square.

"We should go down and have a look; apart from gagging for a pint I am also feeling rather hungry"! the Inspector announced and he led the way down the metal staircase.

-3-

"Hey……….over here you lot"! and a man was standing outside the front porch of the New Tenby House Hotel and he was waving frantically at them. The Inspector and the rest of the ensemble picked up the pace and they trotted over to him.

"Thank God you are here"! the man who was standing upon the front steps of the New Tenby House Hotel told them; and he sounded remarkably genuine. "We have *got* to do something about the pumps down here; it's the same after every pool night; about 8am of the following morning I come down into the bar and I'm always up to my ankles in piss"!

"So what do you want *us* to do about it"?

"You have the yellow flashes upon your shoulders; get your rods and set to work with the unblocking of my drains"!

"What did I tell you"! said DC Wiseman.

"Ah………..I see where you are coming from……but we have actually had a bit of a reorganisation when it comes to the colour coding of the shoulder patches; green is the new sanitation department; we are the yellow peril…….the new and elite killing squad; but as we are here and there has obviously been a bit of a breakdown in communications we will gladly rod your drains for you………….in return for a little hospitality"! Bruno thought aloud and so very quickly that he actually surprised even himself.

"You get in there and help yourselves………you should know where everything is by now; I am just going to pop upstairs and wash my slippers in the tide on North Beach"! said the man who was obviously the landlord of *this* dimension's Tenby House Hotel.

"Your sewers will be safe with us"! Bruno shouted after the landlord as he departed with his slippers. "Blimey………this is a *very* free house"! he said much more quietly.

"Right then…………one drink and then we should try and seek out a kitchen in this establishment"! the Inspector suggested as they entered the premises.

"Up yours, copper"! said the foxy Dr Foxy. "*You* are the only one to be harping on about food; I myself am not that hungry……….and if there is gin in this place then I shall be having that"!

-4-

Rick and Bruno were in the gents toilet; both relieving themselves of several quickly enjoyed pints when they heard the unmistakeable sound of a goodly many feet all running through the courtyard to the side of the hotel and just outside the gents window; and then they heard the front doors to the hotel being thrown open and the many rampaging feet traipsed quickly inward.

"What I would give now for a solid looking suspended ceiling right about now……….there is simply nowhere to hide"! Rick complained; and then the doors to the gents burst open.

"Out"! they were ordered; and with nowhere at all to hide all they could do was comply.

"Which part of *out* do you not understand"? the guard with the green colour coded shoulders wondered of Bruno.

"I am not going anywhere until I have washed my hands"! Bruno explained to the impatient and surly guardsman. "Cleanliness is next to godliness regardless of the dimension; and if it is true that you are indeed setting up a new and Utopian society down here then you will do well to remember the basic rules of hygiene"!

"You have five seconds or I will take you out with my stick"! the guardsman promised.

"I do hope that that is not a toilet orientated euphemism"! Bruno replied; and before his hands were properly dry the impatient and surly guardsman introduced the backs of Bruno's legs to his very whippy length of ash tree.

"Jesus H Christ...........that doesn't half come tight"! Bruno was heard to whimper as Rick picked him up from the floor of the gents and he carried him into the bar area where the

Inspector and the others were sitting down with their hands upon their heads.

"Well now…………what a to-do"! said the man that approached them. He walked with a staff and he was encased in a beige cloak with attached hood and he veritably seemed to glide across the floor of the bar toward them.

"Welcome to Tenby MkII; I am Elder Berry"!

"And where are your friends Dandelion and Burdock"? DC Wiseman wondered; and he too was silenced with the whippy end of an ash branch.

"Ah…………the wit and impetuosity of youth; my name is Berry and I am the leader of the newly elected Tenby MkII town elders……….hence the Elder Berry bit"! and the man removed his hood to reveal a ruddy face that was smiling and quite amenable looking. "Do not let this amenable looking face fool you……….I can be quite the bastard. Now then; tell us for which infernal Government department you spy and we shall send you back to them………..a bit at a time………..over a month or so;

all except for the girl………..she shall be my new family partner"!

"The hell I will"! Dr Foxy protested and she too met up with one of the whippy ash branches.

"We are not Government spies………….and I will thank you never to hurt that lady again"! and the Inspector jumped up and he thumped the two guardsmen who had dared to raise their ash branches against a woman.

Elder Berry was about to call for more guards but the Inspector thumped him as well.

"You *will* hear us out………….and then we will hear *you* out; and then we shall all sit down and have a good and well-mannered chat"! the Inspector told Elder Berry upon whose chest now rested one of his size tens. "Um……….saying that……….we will hear *you* out first"! the Inspector changed his mind and he let Elder Berry get to his feet. "Now………..what is this place and what are you all about"?

"Ah………it would seem that you are not from around here after all"! Elder Berry realised.

"We are from the next parallel dimension over"! the Inspector explained. "We are not at all interested in hurting anybody………or even spying on anyone; we would just like to get home"!

"Oh my goodness………….they only bloody well went and did it then"! Elder Berry realised with a very sad sigh.

"Um…….who went and bloody did *what*"?

"It was a very dark time; there were lots of bad things happening and pretty much all at the same time"! Elder Berry began. "But to cut a long and difficult story short our politicians of the day had us believe that the entire developed world was in the grips of a double-dip recession and that the only way out was in the generation of electricity"!

"Electricity"?

"Yes; the farming and producing of it on vast levels; they poo-pooed the idea of solar and tidal power and they instead opted for the erecting of bloody wind turbines everywhere that it was remotely feasible for a wind turbine to be sited; and not just in this country……………….it was everywhere in the developed world"!

"But I thought that it was common knowledge about the wind turbines not working very well"! the Inspector was fairly convinced.

"Ah yes………..and there lies the irony; they bloody well *don't* work; it is either *too* windy or *not windy enough*. As far as electricity production was concerned everything that this country did was an unbridled flop; but the problem was that it wasn't just us. There were so many bloody turbines all over the bloody place; from here, down through France, Italy, Morocco and Tunisia that during a brief period when they *did* work they just blew the sand and the really hot air up from the Tropics. Not long after the one millionth turbine started turning Britain was turned into a desert wasteland in a couple of months; and that was pretty much the end of civilisation as we knew it. The desert very quickly enveloped everything and we decided to abandon our homes to the relentless sand and to move underground"!

"Um………you shared with us a bit of a *eureka* moment earlier on and you mentioned something about *them* doing it…..or words to that effect"! the Inspector reminded Elder Berry. "So………*who* did *what*, exactly"?

"That sorry collection of lying, cheating and scheming corrupt politicians of our day; it was rumoured that their technical people had found a way of travelling between dimensions; and they wanted to find a dimension that was very similar to our own so that they could set up their wind turbines again…….albeit slightly differently; so that *this time* they could get the distribution right and prove that they had not been wrong; it is all about saving face with that bloody lot of tossers"!

"So; assuming what you say is correct…….and that they have *indeed* found a way of travelling between dimensions; and that Woodfield Grove in Cosheston is their gateway thing; then they must have killed the two Germans because they followed the solar panel way of thinking and they were seen as a threat to the bloody wind turbines. Well……….a murder is a murder no matter *what* dimension it is committed in……….and I promise that I will bring these people to justice"!

"Do you know………..but with your exacting moral standards you might well be the person who can do this"! Elder Berry said with a smile.

"But first we have to get back to our own dimension"! the Inspector was sure. "I have troops back there who need the rallying"!

"Ah……."!

Chapter Ten

"You should at least stay for the night; rest a while and start with your travelling in the morning when you are all feeling better and refreshed"! Elder Berry pleaded with the Inspector and he winked at the others in the vain hope that one of them might agree with him and adopt his stance.

"Thank you for your very kind offer; but I am a firm believer in there being no time like the present"! and the Inspector sounded as though his mind was quite made up.

"Oh; believe you me………you do *not* want to be in the open desert after it gets dark"! Rick told the Inspector; and Rick's face was the most serious that he could possibly make it. "Things live in the sand; nocturnal things………nocturnal things that would probably wish you harm"!

"What sort of things……….little sand-hopping bugs is it"? the Inspector derided.

"No; bloody big wand worms actually"! Elder Berry informed the Inspector. "They are great big things the size of houses; we have seen them from a distance..........but nobody who has got any closer has ever lived to tell the tale"!

"Sand worms"?

"Aye; great vicious brutes with jaws that open four ways to show a *huge* ring of teeth........and intestinal tracts that are rank with the stench of death; these beasts are *definitely* not the herbivores"!

"Perhaps an early night and a bit of a rest might be just what the doctor ordered"! the Inspector mused.

"That's more like it; besides...........tonight is fun quiz night in Tenby MkII House; it would be a shame for you to miss out"!

"I am absolutely convinced that they are nocturnal"! Rick seemed fairly sure as they stood within the entrance to the boarded up Sun Inn the very next morning. "You can feel them moving round underneath your feet at night; but I have never once felt that during the day!" and Rick was telling the Inspector everything that he knew about the sand worms. "But if it happens that you *do* feel something moving around in the sand underneath your feet then just stand still………the worms seem to be attracted by all rhythmic movement"!

"This is getting a bit like that film *Tremors* with Kevin Bacon"! DC Wiseman was sure.

"You are wrong; Rick and I have *both* caught glimpses of the passing of these sand worms………..and it is *much* more like *Dune* with Kyle MacLachlan"! Bruno was sure.

They trudged very warily up the dune and away from Tenby MkII; hopefully in the direction that would take them to the railway station.

When they reached the top of the dune they all breathed a sigh of relief as they saw the station beneath them where the silver bullet train waited for them.

"To Cosheston……..and hopefully not beyond"! the Inspector said quite cheerfully.

"All aboard"! said The Bluns.

-3-

"Do you know………..but I think that this is going to be an awful lot easier that I at first thought"! the Inspector said with a smile as they climbed down from the train and they stood upon the sand in front of the small and rural station. "Our footprints of yesterday are still in the sand; we should be able to retrace our footsteps straight back to number thirteen Woodfield Grove"!

"And then what"? Rick had good cause to wonder. "You have surely not forgotten about number thirteen and the disappearing gateway thing"!

"Ah…………I have a plan when it comes to number thirteen and the disappearing gateway thing; thanks to a little help from Elder Berry………and *this*"! and the Inspector brandished the physical element to his plan.

"Is that a stick of bloody dynamite"?

"That it is"!

"But if you blow up the gateway thing then we might never be able to get home"! Dr Foxy worried. "Have you properly thought this through"?

"Aha………..my plan is not to blow the gateway thing up; using the stick of dynamite as supplied by Elder Berry I am merely going to agitate the gateway thing's surrounding molecules"! the Inspector tried to explain to the quizzical faces. "You see………the gateway thing is still there; it is just cleverly disguised on a molecular level. By agitating the surrounding molecules with the type of sudden shock that a stick of dynamite can produce the kitchen and the gateway thing will become visible again; but probably not for very long so we shall have to be quick………..and that much is probably just as well because

Elder Berry is almost certain that the blast will attract the sand worms…………the really *big* sand worms"!

"Well that's good; so if the gateway thing doesn't reappear then the sand worms will get us"! and Bruno pointed out what he thought to be the flaw in the Inspector's plan.

"Then we will just have to hope that the dynamite *does* work………..you should have a little faith"! the Inspector encouraged everyone. "Now then……….has anybody got a light of any kind; my Zippo is back in the other dimension and I think that I left my box of matches on the bar in Tenby House MkII"!

-4-

"So……….what is the plan for the dynamite; are you going to light it and throw it from here"? Bruno wondered as they stood at the top of the dune and they stared down to where they hoped number thirteen was located.

"No………..a little bit too inaccurate; we shall all have to get a bit nearer and then I shall carefully place the dynamite just where Elder Berry told me to place the dynamite……..and then I shall run for cover"! and the Inspector explained the finer points of his plan.

"Run for cover………..*where*; it's open desert down there and there isn't much in the way of any cover"! and Rick thought that he had better point as much out.

"That much has just occurred to me as well"! the Inspector admitted as he looked all around for the slightest bit of inspiration. "Give me a hand to lift one of those wooden tables from the platform of the rural station. We can upend it and stick it in the sand a short distance from the proposed blast site and we can all hide behind it. It is only *one* stick of dynamite………..the blast won't be *that* big"!

Ten minutes later the upended table was in place and they were all hiding behind it; all except for The Bluns who had gone back to his previous role as conductor on his precious train; and the Inspector who was about to do daring things with the stick of dynamite.

"Right then………….it's time to get this party started"! the Inspector was sure and he gripped his stick of dynamite and Dr Foxy's lighter and he ran to where he thought the stick of dynamite should be placed.

"He has lit it…………and now he is running this way"! and the foxy Dr Foxy was providing the running commentary. "I should get your heads down if I were you"!

The Inspector leapt over the upended table and he huddled up close to the others who all had their eyes shut and their fingers in their ears. The countdown was running in the Inspector's head; three…..two…..one; and exactly on cue there was a loud bang as the dynamite went up and sand was blasted in all directions.

They all peered over the top of the upended table and they tried to make out what, if anything, had happened; and as the sand cloud slowly started to dissipate they soon started to make out the shape of something in the middle distance.

"Thar she blows………………..what did I tell you"! the Inspector shouted as he pointed out the kitchen to number thirteen. "Come on……….look lively you lot"!

"Um……..if I were you I would look *very* bloody lively"! Rick was sure as he sprinted ahead of the others. "Can you feel the movement in the sand; the bloody worms are coming"!

Spurred on by his advice the others all leapt to their feet and they started running toward the kitchen at number thirteen; which was no easy feat now that there was so much movement in the ground beneath their feet. Dr Foxy with Bruno helping her were the last to arrive in the kitchen when something huge and black erupted from the sand only thirty yards behind them; its roar almost deafening when added to the sound like rushing wind that its segmented body was making as the giant sand monster rocketed across the sand toward them.

"Quickly; down the hallway and out of the front door"! the Inspector shouted over the hideous cacophony. "As soon as we are out the front door then that should be an end to it"!

They dashed along the hallway and they threw themselves out of the front door; landing in a heap on the ornamental gravel between the many pots of azaleas and the box balls. The roaring of the giant sand worm could still be heard on the other side of the front door; but the worm stayed safely on the other side.

"Well thank *Christ* for that; I never thought that I would ever be so glad to see Woodfield Grove again"! said the Inspector with a very nervous sounding edge to his voice. "Come on then; we have to get down to the Station and round up some reinforcements"!

"What do we need reinforcements for"?

"So we can come back here and arrest every member of Woodfield Grove for murder, conspiring to pervert the course of justice, stepping on the cracks in the pavement; every single charge, trumped up or otherwise, that I can throw at these people. And when *that* is done we shall see what can be done about stopping their bloody wind turbines"!

Chapter Eleven

"Where is the Super"?

"Search me"! the Desk Sergeant invited them.

"Right then…………this is the situation; there is an on-going armed siege in Cosheston; and before you ask……. you ask……*yes, another one*; but this time it is in Woodfield Grove. I need armed response units and as many uniforms as can be awoken"! and the Inspector was selectively sparing when it came to the whole truth. "Oh……….and helicopters; better thrown in a few helicopters as well"!

"And you of course have all the relevant paperwork to authorise such an undertaking"! the Desk Sergeant replied rather too sarcastically for the Inspector's liking.

"You should know me better than to talk about the paperwork"!

"Ah…………..then I had better try and get in touch with the Super"! the Desk Sergeant presumed. "He will have to authorise all of this; and we might even have to go as high as the Deputy Chief Constable if you are really intent on having the helicopters"!

"So the Super is not in the building then"! the Inspector gleaned from the response of the Desk Sergeant.

"No Inspector; I would imagine him to be somewhere around the fourteenth by now"!

"Would there happen to be anybody in the building who is above the rank of Inspector"?

"No Sir"!

"Then as this is an emergency and I am the highest ranking officer in the house then *I* am authorising it……..the helicopters as well; and you had better make it all happen before any civilian lives are lost"!

"He is only playing in Pembroke Dock, Inspector……and I have his mobile number; it will take less than a minute and he can be here in less than ten"! the Desk Sergeant promised and it was then that DC Wiseman introduced the Desk Sergeant to his whippy length of ash tree that he had smuggled out of Tenby MkII down his trouser leg.

"He is one of them"! DC Wiseman was shouting as he did for the Desk Sergeant.

"Um………..that probably wouldn't be a very good idea; the armed response units and the helicopters and everything"! said Rick as he and Bruno suddenly appeared on the scene.

"Bloody hell………..I have only just realised that you have not been with us much ever since we crashed back through that front door"! the Inspector suddenly realised. "Where on earth did the pair of you get to"?

"Stand down the units, Sergeant Adams"!

"Yes Sir Mr Dylan Sir"!

"What the bloody hell is going on; are you in league with that *other* lot"?

"Um………we should probably take a walk in the car park"! Rick suggested.

"And what is with all of this *yes sir Mr Dylan sir crap*"? the Inspector *also* wondered.

"All will be revealed"!

-2-

"So then………." the Inspector wondered as he lit a cigarette. "*Whose* pocket are *you two* in; *whose* side are *you* on then"?

"There is no question……….we are on *your* side; this is *our* world as well. You know me to be a lifelong resident of Cosheston……………you have been friendly with my mum and dad since I started crawling; and when I was thinking about all of this when we were running away from that nasty sand worm something suddenly occurred to me………..the people that I know up in Woodfield Grove have lived there longer than I have been alive"! Rick started to explain.

"Many of them longer than me as well"! the Inspector added.

"Exactly; so there is no reason to believe that the gateway thing is a relatively *recent* thing; that lot have probably been coming and going for years"!

"No; that is impossible; I would have noticed"! the Inspector was sure.

"But *would* you have noticed though; the rumours of wife swapping were just that……..rumours; and they have done *nothing* else to draw any attention to themselves. The houses up in the Grove were built in the early fifties; and the bungalows, of which number thirteen is obviously one, went up some ten years later; and for as long as *I* have been around the very same people have lived in those houses……..apart from a few natural deaths associated with longevity; so it is very feasible that these people have been coming and going for as long as that"! Rick hypothesised.

"But why"?

"I can only offer one suggestion; look………..the technology behind wind turbines is quite new as far as *we* are concerned; but what if that lot in the next parallel dimension over have been in possession of that sort of technology for donkey's years. What if they already realised that they dropped a bit of a bollock as long ago as our 1950's and they used their gateway thing to open up their dimension with Woodfield Grove back then. Elder Berry has already told us that their politicians wanted to prove that they had not been wrong when it came to the wind turbines by sticking them up in *our* dimension as well……..but that sort of thing cannot be done overnight. Those involved in the politics of Woodfield Grove would have to wheedle themselves into positions of power and influence……….some of them would not even have lived long enough to see that through and it is now their *children* who are now occupying such positions; but with the way that permission is now being granted to such turbines more and more frequently then I would say that their infernal plan is reaching some sort of fruition"!

"Yours is indeed the frightening scenario"! the Inspector said quite gravely. "And once again we find ourselves in the position of not knowing just who we can trust; and it doesn't have to stop with Woodfield Grove; their members could be anywhere in the County…………….the *Country* even"!

"There is no reason to stop there; from what I have heard about them I am thinking total world domination"! Rick suggested. "Anyway; to that end Bruno and I have whooshed about in time a bit and we have formed a team of people that we *know* are to be trusted because we have worked with them before"! and Rick nodded in the direction of the ten black vans that were parked over the road in Asda's car park.

"Who are your friends"?

"Why don't you come over and say hello……….I feel quite sure that you will like them"!

"Right then………..before we go *any* further I think it only pertinent to make it widely known that I have absolutely *no* desire to be cut down and killed in a hail of American bloody friendly fire"! the Inspector said to Agent Statler and his men who were all *very* American. "I do not think that there is anything even *remotely* friendly about the accidental shooting of one's own comrades………..and maybe it should really be called *gung-ho poorly educated incompetent fire*"!

"None taken"! said Agent Statler when it came to any possible offence.

"Look…………..have you ever seen that TV show Primeval where the secret quasi-autonomous Government department go around shooting dinosaurs and the like that have managed to crawl through anomalies in the space-time continuum"? Rick wondered of the Inspector. "That really pretty bird from S Club7 is in it"!

"I have been forced to endure it once or twice; but only because I suspect my young son has a crush on that very girl"!

"Well; unfortunately that TV show is just the stuff of fantasy……..the schoolboy crush *and* the whole secret quasi-autonomous Government department; Britain does not *have* such a department…………….but America *does*"! Rick pointed out. "More often than not this American department just polices improprieties in time……….but they are fully equipped to deal with the dimension jumping as well; and we also really need their help"!

"Gentlemen; you know that I would be lying if I said that we weren't in any great trouble"! Agent Statler spoke and he sounded completely unfazed by the Inspector's previous outburst as they sat in the back of the largest black van that had a table and some soft chairs around it; and there was even a drink's trolley. "Getting the dimension jumping miscreants out of Cosheston and back through the gateway thing to their own dimension is going to be the easy part; but it's knowing how further afield their rot has set in is going to be a bit more tricky; but I would suggest that we set this ball rolling by ridding Cosheston of its menace first and then destroying the gateway thing………..the rest of the World we can concentrate on later. Astoria…………pedal to the metal, son; let's get started"!

"Yes Sir; wagons are rolling"! Agent Astoria said over his walkie-talkie which was code for the other black vans to start moving.

"How about if we stormed Woodfield Grove, sent them all back through the gateway thing but we kept one of them prisoner"? DC Wiseman suggested.

"Aha………..I *do* like the way that you think, young Detective Constable; we could quite easily do that"! Agent Statler seemed quite sure. "We could extract *all* sorts of information from a suitably prepared prisoner………just as long as you Brits don't keep harping on about his or her human rights"!

"I don't think that anybody else need know"! the Inspector sounded convinced. "Although you and your men will have to try your hardest not to prematurely kill the detainee with your incessant friendly fire"!

"Touché…………and your point is duly taken. Now then; this is what we shall do………..and have you ever seen *this* man"? and Agent Statler handed a couple of photographs to the Inspector and DC Wiseman.

"As a matter of fact I have"! and the Inspector was convinced of as much. "I have seen him walking a dog around the village……..a spaniel I think; and I think that I might even have seen him in the pub from time to time. I don't know his name though……..he seems to keep himself pretty much to himself"!

"Intelligence would have us believe that this man is known colloquially as Phil the Shed; and we think it likely that he is fairly high up in their ranks"! Agent Statler explained. "If the opportunity arises then this man shall be our detainee……..so keep your eyes peeled; half an hour of waterboarding should have him singing like a canary"!

"In position Sir"! Agent Astoria informed Statler and the others.

"What…………*already*; in position *where*"?

"In Cosheston Sir………….at the bottom of Woodfield Grove; we have an excellent view of number thirteen from here and there is a fella walking down the road with his dog that you should probably be very interested in………..the fella that is, and not the dog"!

"Oh my goodness...........I *love* it when a plan comes together"! Agent Statler exclaimed with some glee as he clapped eyes upon the one man and his dog. "Bag him"!

-3-

"I am afraid that I do not have the time to help you with your survey or whatever it is you happen to be doing; I have a beef and homemade red wine casserole in the oven; not to mention my slow-baked brown bread doggie treats"! Phil the Shed pointed out.

"Like it or not.............you *will* help"! and Phil the Shed was dragged from the street and manhandled into the back of the largest of the black vans.

"I am sure that various of my human rights are being violated and/or abused"! Phil the Shed was sure as a hessian sack was pulled over his head. "Not to mention what could happen to an unattended beef casserole and a tray of slow-baked brown bread doggie treats"!

"Right………forget all about your God-damned beef casserole; let us instead talk about your God-damned wind turbines; the transgression of dimensions and the murder of two German solar panel surveyors"! Agent Statler insisted.

"Oh my *God*………….are you Americans"? Phil the Shed gasped underneath his hessian sack. "I would just like to make it quite clear that I have reached this ripe old age without *once* having come close to being done for in a hail of friendly fire; even the name for such a thing sounds quite preposterous"!

"Astoria………….turn on the taps"!

"Yes Sir"!

"Is that the sound of running water; I could really do with a wee right about now"! Phil the Shed protested as the water cascaded over the hessian sack where it covered his face. "Hasn't waterboarding been outlawed and banned in this dimension"?

"Aha……"!

"Oh crap"!

"Start talking names and addresses"!

"Over my dead body"!

"If you insist"!

"Up yours, American copper; you can put me back through the gateway just before you destroy it forever……….and that is probably the extent of your piss-poor planning; I will take my chances on the other side with the sand worms"!

"Are you sure; you won't stand much of a chance on the other side"! Agent Statler was more or less honest. "Those sand worms are pretty riled up in there……….and we will certainly not be making it at all easy for you"!

"Your puny threats do not frighten me"! Phil the Shed was sure. "Do your pitiful worst"!

"You cannot be bloody serious"! complained Phil the Shed. "What sort of a sicko dreamed up something like *this*"?

"I have been told that I have one of those minds"! DC Wiseman admitted.

Phil the Shed's wrists were locked either side of his head within a sort of a yolk affair; and upon his back DC Wiseman and Agent Astoria had rather cleverly mounted a battery powered portable hi-fi with some impressive looking speakers that pointed straight at the ground.

"A bit of Rage against the Machine should get those worms nicely interested"! Agent Astoria was sure.

"Would these musicians happen to play a heavily bass orientated and rhythmic style of music"? Agent Statler honestly wondered for he was not that *up* on the music of the day.

"That they do"!

"This is tantamount to murder"! Phil the Shed was sure. "I thought that it was your public obligation to *uphold* the law"?

"We are a non-Government operation"!

"What; sort of like a quango"?

"That is enough of the maudlin talk of quangos and the like; time to move out"! and Agent Statler threw Phil the Shed out of the side door of the biggest and blackest of the trucks and onto the pavement. "I take it that we are good to go"? Statler double checked with Astoria.

"We are *indeed* good to go; the batteries are brand new and are glued in; the dials and everything are all set and glued solid; all *we* have to do is hit the play button on the remote control and we'll soon be belting out *Wake Up* by Rage at maximum decibels"! Astoria was happy to report.

"Wake Up………..how appropriate; although the sand worms will be the *least* of your worries"! Agent Statler told Phil the Shed. "No; you should be more worried about the thirty or so of your comrades that we will be sending back with you. Some of the boys were thinking about having a sweepstake for when it comes to how long they will let you live………..but as we won't be there to see then it is a bit of a moot point"!

"You are a twisted psycho"!

"Thank you for that; now get up and start walking"!

Rick and Bruno and Dr Foxy walked up the right hand side of the street with the assigned American Agents and they used cattle prods to keep the procession of other-dimension people moving in the right direction toward number thirteen; while the Inspector, DC Wiseman, Statler and Astoria all marched up the other side of the street and they were similarly armed.

"What's that on Phil's back"? a number of the other-dimension people wondered.

"I'm not sure………….but if I were to guess then I would say that it is a portable ghetto-blaster"! one of the other-dimension people seemed sure.

"Holy shit……….if that is the case then they know all about the sand worms and their attraction to rhythmic disturbances"! another of the unwelcome guests realised. "If they turn *that* thing on then the worms will *surely* come; we will have to kill him and use his body as a decoy while we sprint to the train"!

"Can you hear all of the murmurings; they are already plotting your downfall"! Agent Statler whispered to Phil the Shed. "Names and addresses………….that is all it would take to secure your release"!

"I shall say it again………..up yours, American copper"!

The guarded conversations and murmurings of the others all stopped and the procession slowed as they were herded, single file and in silence, in through the garden gate to number thirteen. Their manacles were released as each of them passed through the front door and they were poked with cattle prods to ensure that they kept going in the right direction whether they needed reminding or not.

"One last chance"! Agent Statler checked with Phil the Shed.

"Nothing you say shall change my mind"!

"Then we shall say goodbye"! and Agent Statler *himself* released the manacles about Phil the Shed's ankles; and he footed the man's backside lest the electrical cattle prods damaged the mini hi-fi.

"Agent Astoria………..some mood music if you please; Rick……….tie this rope around my waist and for the love of God do not let go"!

Phil the Shed was the last of the captives to enter the dimension jumping portal; and even though he was nowhere to be seen those upon the front porch could all hear Rage Against The Machine in all their stereophonic glory. Agent Statler took up a rifle that had been slung over his shoulder; and as he inched closer to the kitchen and the gateway he prepared to fire.

"What is he doing"? Bruno was heard to wonder.

Statler fired into the kitchen; but the resultant blast was not heard in the Woodfield Grove of *this* dimension; and Rick gathered up the slack in the rope and he reeled in Agent Statler.

"Rocket propelled grenade"! Agent Astoria explained to Bruno. "I think that he is making sure the sand worms really *do* turn up"!

From the front door to number thirteen they all heard the roar of the sand worms and the shrieks and cries and howls of the unwelcome guests. Very soon the shrieks and cries and howls were no more and the roaring of the sand worms diminished as the worms travelled further and further away from the portal; and then Rage Against The Machine stopped very abruptly.

"Right……………we need to destroy this gateway thing so that their kind never make it back through"! the Inspector was sure.

"Not just yet"! Agent Statler was sure.

"Come again; I thought that this was all agreed"!

"Yes; we *do* need to close this gateway………but what we also need to do is to stop their kind who are already in our dimension from turning our world into a barren wasteland as well; and I think that we can only do that properly from in there"! and Agent Statler nodded toward the kitchen. "But I think that we should wait a while until we are sure that the worms have properly gone"!

Chapter Twelve

-1-

"So............what is it actually like in there"? Agent Statler was the first of the Americans to ask as they reconvened their little confab in the back of the biggest of the big and black trucks.

"Well.........it's hard to explain; like I said there is an awful lot of sand; and apart from the sand there isn't that much to write home about..........save for the railway affair and the town that is newly created yet buried under the sand at the same time"! Rick tried his best to explain.

"A train............in the middle of a desert"? and Agent Astoria was somewhat taken aback.

"It certainly beats riding a camel"! DC Wiseman told Astoria.

"Oh yes…………one of those little silver bullet train jobs; and it hasn't always been desert; the desert is a relatively recent thing"! Bruno reminded the Americans.

"So where does this railroad go; is there a timetable that you can have a look at"?

"There doesn't seem to be a timetable anywhere that *we* have seen; you just sort of take the train yourself if you want to go somewhere; but to where it goes other than to Tenby MkII we are at a bit of a loss"!

"But there are people living in this Tenby MkII"?

"Oh yes…………they've got a pub and everything"! Bruno was quick to add.

"And the people there seem as friendly as; just as soon as they have ascertained that you are not the spies sent by the Government that they so obviously despise"!

"Then this Tenby MkII shall be where we shall start……..first thing tomorrow morning………sand worms willing. We shall take this bullet train of which you have told us and we shall speak with these people; find out if *they* know where else this bullet train goes other than just their town; and if they are worried about Government spies then it stands to reason that their Government's Headquarters are not that far away"!

"All aboard"! said The Bluns and he did wave his flag and blow upon his whistle. "Blimey............*this* is certainly going to be a standing room only job"! he commented as he regarded the stream of men in black suits that emerged from the inter-dimensional gateway.

"And who the hell is *this*"? Agent Statler wondered of The Bluns; and Statler's hand was preparing to draw his pistol from its shoulder holster.

"Ah; don't you worry about The Bluns; he is sort of with us"! and Rick explained as best he could.

"But he is wearing a conductor's uniform of sorts; does *he* not know to where this train goes other than Tenby MkII"?

"Nah; he's not from around here; he used to be our postman years ago…………..and there is also the fact that he appears to have gone a bit bonkers; between you and me I think that it might be due to LSD flashbacks or something; all we know is………he is called The Bluns"!

"Because his surname is Blunsden"? Agent Statler correctly assumed.

"That is pretty much the long and the short of it; now……..the train is just over the top of this first sand dune; and please instruct your men not to run or jump around………..the vibrations would surely attract the worms"!

"The name *Blunsden* is strangely familiar to me"! Agent Statler seemed both puzzled and sure and both at the same time. "Remind me to check it out when we get back"!

"I admire your optimism"!

"So do I"!

"This is indeed a very fine train"! Agent Statler remarked as they climbed aboard and he found himself instantly in the good books belonging to The Bluns. "So.........how far away is this Tenby MkII place"?

"Well..........it's sort of hard to tell"! DC Wiseman answered Agent Statler. "We have to go underground for most of the way; but it doesn't take much longer than ten minutes"! and DC Wiseman started the train moving.

In both carriages and in every seat men in black suits checked their weapons and their supplies of ammunition as the train hurtled through the dark.

"Next stop will be Tenby MkII"! DC Wiseman announced. "I can see a little light at the end of the tunnel; it shouldn't be long at all now"!

The train came to a halt at the station and the men in black followed the same route as the Inspector and the others; which was exactly the same route as they had walked the day before;

over the footbridge, up the sand dune and then down the other side; and it wasn't very long before they were all huddled behind the bar of the boarded up Sun Inn and staring at the wall that had just revealed a lift.

"I should be amongst the first party to go down; these people already know me and although their weapons are quite rudimentary they can certainly come quite tight if they suspect that you are the Government spies"! and the Inspector explained his way of thinking.

"That makes sense to me; so………..you Inspector, DC Wiseman and Dr Foxy shall come down with Astoria and myself and the rest of the first party; Rick………..you accompany the second party; Bruno……….you come down with the last lot"! Agent Statler decided. "That way if we get split up for any reason then each party will have a leader who knows their way around down there"!

"That makes sense" Rick and Bruno both agreed.

"Right then; let's do this"! Agent Statler decided and the Inspector pressed at the only button upon the wall and the lift doors went *ping*.

-4-

"Just look at it; this is now getting *way* beyond a joke.......I am well and truly up to my ankles in piss"! the Landlord of the New Tenby House Hotel was shouting from his front doorstep. His slippers were in his hands again; and this time his trousers were rolled half way up to his knees. "Oh; it's you again"! the Landlord also said as he recognised the faces of Rick and Bruno and a few of the others. "You seem to have come somewhat mob-handed this time"!

"We would speak to Elder Berry"! the Inspector told the grumpy publican without displaying anything in the way of any emotion. "I trust that you can make this happen"!

"I can arrange that for you; but do me a big favour and mention to him the problems that I am having me my drains" the

Landlord pleaded of them. "That Elder Berry doesn't seem to take much notice of my protestations"!

"Consider it done"!

With barely enough time having passed for the smoking of a quick cigarette the Inspector found himself sitting around the largest table that the New Tenby House Hotel had to offer; and he was in the company of DC Wiseman, Rick and Bruno, the lovely Dr Foxy and Agents Statler and Astoria.

"Can anybody else smell wee"? the Inspector wondered.

"Ah……..my apologies; it always gets a bit like this after pool or quiz night"! Elder Berry apologised. "That reminds me………I must have my resident surveyors look at the sewage pumps that we have installed; they are obviously not up to the job"!

"Thank you"! the Landlord silently mouthed from the door to the kitchen.

"So…………this neat little train of yours; where does it go"? and Agent Statler steered the conversation away from the issue of the drains and the inadequate sewage pumps.

"Oh………that train is not of *our* making; and we do not really know that much about it……..other than it is popular with the Government spies"! Elder Berry was nothing if not completely honest. "But……….if you were upon the train and you were to head back in the direction in which you came then God only knows where you would end up; but we do know that if you carry on from here you will end up in the capital"!

"What………..London"?

"No…………..Cardiff; our capital that *used to be*; provided that you make it alive past the sand people of the outer desert; I have heard that they are quite the ruthless lot"!

"There are sand *people* to go with the sand *worms*"?

"A lawless and renegade bunch with little in the way of any scruples"!

"Please do not tell me that these sand people have blue within blue eyes"! DC Wiseman asked not to be told.

"Well; I suppose that statistically speaking *some* of them will have blue eyes"! Elder Berry was sure and also looking rather perplexed.

"You haven't seen *Dune* then"? Wiseman surmised.

"Dune what"?

"*Dune* the movie...........with Kyle MacLachlan"!

"I must have missed that one"!

"Do these sand people ride around on the back of the giant sand worms"?

"Are you kidding; the worms would have them for breakfast"!

"Then we should be safe"! DC Wiseman seemed sure. "Unless they *do* ride around on the back of the worms when you are not looking and they have developed an army whose weapons are based on sound"!

"What"?

"Anyway........." said Agent Statler as he tried his utmost to reclaim the conversation that he had initiated. "What would we find in this place you call Cardiff.........if we were to venture there"?

"The remnants of the Governments………those bastards"! and Elder Berry spat upon the floor of the bar.

"Then to Cardiff it is"! Agent Statler was sure.

"Now then; neither too fast nor too slow……..is it possible you can do something in the middle"? Agent Statler wondered of DC Wiseman as the doors to the train swished almost silently closed and the silver bullet train started to pull away from the station at Tenby MkII.

"I think I can manage that"!

"And kill these internal lights; it will be easier to spot an ambush if we are dark inside"!

"Um…………I don't think that I can turn them off; but they operate on a dimmer so I will turn them down as far as they can go"! Wiseman promised.

"Then that will have to do; and the same for this piped music if you please"!

Under the control of DC Wiseman the bullet train pulled away from the station at Tenby MkII and it picked up a goodly amount of speed in a very short space of time; so much so that it fairly *blasted* into the sand tunnel.

"Do you think that these sand tunnels are entirely safe"? Agent Astoria was heard to wonder. "I mean...........you hear tragic stories all the time about kids being buried alive while on their holidays because they've been digging tunnels on the beach"!

Several of the black suited agents who had until now been sitting in the carriage fiddling with and cleaning their guns stopped what they were doing to look at Agent Astoria, and then at the darkness that was outside the windows, before switching their attention back to Agent Astoria once again.

"I am sure that they would not have built them if there was any chance that they were not safe; this train is itself primarily used by their Government"! Agent Statler was sure and he spoke loud enough so that the agents in both of the carriages would surely have heard him; which they obviously did for guns were back to being ferociously cleaned once again.

"I don't know so much; they certainly dropped a bit of a bollock when it came to all of their wind turbines"! Astoria interjected.

"Because this train and the tunnels and everything were obviously put in place *after* the great wind turbine fiasco, when hopefully they might have learnt a bit of a lesson"!

"Here we go; I can see light up ahead and that surely means the end of the tunnel"! DC Wiseman informed everybody aboard; and throughout both carriages there were many sighs of relief sighed. "I am going to start slowing down a bit just in case"!

The train burst out of the tunnel and the train's windows did a wonderful job of automatically tinting and cutting out the glare.

"Blimey………...some *more* of the seaside"! DC Wiseman noticed as he stared out of the tinted glass of the driver's compartment.

"Indeed……………but it is a seaside with a difference"! and the Inspector was pointing here and there. "Look at all of the industrial type scars upon the landscape and the remains of the falling down road bridges in the distance; I think that this might be *this* dimension's take on the Port Talbot that we know"!

"I wonder if it *smells* as bad as the Port Talbot that we know"? Bruno wondered.

"We will soon have the chance to find out"! DC Wiseman sounded sure. "There is something blocking the track just up ahead; and that means that some of us will have to get out and move said obstruction. It is probably a good thing that I slowed the train down otherwise we might have been derailed"!

"This might well be a trap; you see it all the time in the old westerns"! the Inspector worried.

"I sure as hell can't see anyone out there"! Agent Statler was mostly sure. "Right then men.........."! And Agent Statler did his best to divert the attention of his agents away from the cleaning of their guns. "I want you to split yourselves into two groups..........we shall call these groups over thirties and under thirties. Those of you still in your twenties shall be the lifting party to clear the obstruction; everybody else shall stand guard and I should like that to include at least two snipers on the roof of both carriages. Wiseman………..the doors if you please"!

"Um…………I don't think that doing that would be a very wise move at the moment"! and DC Wiseman pointed at the vast wall of sand that was approaching from what would have been the north in their own dimension. "I think that we are about to be hit by a sandstorm or something"!

"Jesus H Christ……………that is indeed a sandstorm and a half"! Statler was sure. "Well get your pedal to the metal boy and get us back in that tunnel"!

"That much has already occurred to me"! DC Wiseman was honest. "And believe me when I say that I am trying to do just that; it's just that we don't seem to be moving. The computer on the dashboard says that I am in reverse and the brakes are off………but moving we are definitely not"!

"Theo………..open one of the doors for a minute before the sandstorm hits us"! the Inspector asked of DC Wiseman. "Something that I know of this place in *our* dimension has me worried"!

DC Wiseman opened the door nearest to the Inspector and he jumped down onto the sand; and after a cursory examination of the underside of the train the Inspector climbed back aboard and Wiseman closed the door from the fast approaching storm.

"It is as I suspected; we have been stopped in Port Talbot for only a matter of a few minutes and already we are up on bricks and somebody has had away with our wheels"! the Inspector announced.

"You're shitting me; I didn't even see anyone"! and Agent Statler was quite flabbergasted. "Not even in New Jersey are the thieves so quick; were it not for the inconvenience then I would be quite impressed"!

"Now then; do we sit tight and ride out the storm in here……..or should we try to run back to the tunnel on foot"? the Inspector wondered. "The tunnel is surely not that far behind us"!

"The storm is coming in very quickly Sir"! Wiseman was sure. "You can't even see the remains of the bridges anymore; I'm not sure whether we would make it back to the tunnel on time"! and as DC Wiseman was speaking his wise words the first grains of sand started to blast against the windows of the train.

"You are right; and it does look as though we are stuck here for the time being"! the Inspector realised just what Agent Statler had been thinking. "At least we are out of the storm and we have some light on the matter"!

"And now might be a good time to break out the provisions that Elder Berry provided for us"! Agent Statler was sure. "We can't be doing much of anything else for a while so we might as well have us some lunch"!

"Well…………..looking at this little lot there doesn't appear to be any shortage of Bourbon and chips in Tenby MkII"! Agent Statler noticed as Bruno unpacked the box that contained their packed lunches and they all stared at the many bottles of whisky and the four multi-packs of assorted crisps.

"Not being familiar with this place we don't know just how long this storm is going to rage for; now might be a goodly time for everybody to have a little drink and then maybe a bit of a nap; we don't know when the next chance to have a rest might present itself"! the Inspector suggested.

"I can appreciate the logic in what you are saying"! Agent Statler afforded the Inspector. "I don't suppose that you have happened across an ice making machine anywhere on this train, have you"?

"Right..........I have left the train in gear"! and DC Wiseman came bounding along the aisle just as soon as he heard that there was Bourbon in the offing. "The doors cannot be opened from inside or out when the train is in gear...........and I don't think that we're going to be accidentally rushing off anywhere..........what with us being up on bricks and everything"!

"I have found some glasses"! Bruno piped up with the box of glasses still in his arms. "We should get this party started"!

"It is definitely *not* a party"!

"Oh yes...........then we should get this purely-in-the-line-of-the-job-pre-operation-nap started"! Bruno conceded.

"That is better"! Agent Statler told him. "I don't suppose you found an ice making machine when you came across those glasses"?

"No; we'll all have to have it straight and neat"! Bruno bore the sad news as he broke the seal on the first bottle of Bourbon. "And please give any prawn cocktail flavour crisps to those that might actually like them or are too hungry to care"!

Chapter Thirteen

-1-

"Well…………there's the first dead man"! Bruno slurred and he tossed the empty bottle that had once held Bourbon into the metal waste bin; and his throwing of the bottle caused such an unholy clattering and banging that nobody upon the train was able to hear anything other than the empty bottle rattling around in the metal waste bin; which then promptly fell over"!

If Bruno had not been making such an unholy racket then those upon the double carriage bullet train might well have been aware of the strange noises that were coming from underneath the train; but thanks to Bruno they didn't and so they carried on with their drinking of neat bourbon in some ignorance.

"Do you know…………but I was about to start wondering whether this American phenomenon of the friendly fire was at all alcohol related"? the Inspector wondered; and it looked as though the drinking of neat whisky wasn't helping very much when it came to the stability of his own feet. "But it seems as though most of your men are already asleep; you Yanks are quite the lightweights when it comes to the drinking of whisky"! the Inspector sniggered.

"I can assure you that they are not normally like this; in certain circles we are known as the *beer disposal unit*........and that also takes in all manner of wines and spirits as well"! Agent Statler was sure and equally proud of as much. "Astoria........go about the carriages and wake them all up; this is doing our reputation no good at all"!

"I would like to, Sir............but nothing I can do will make my legs return to their previous workings; and I am *so* sleepy as well"! Astoria yawned; and then he mumbled something before he fell fast asleep.

"I smell a rat"! Agent Statler was sure. "A rat in the form of nerve gas or something very similar"!

Agent Statler tried to get out of his own chair; but his legs had very recently taken to the understanding that they had been fashioned from lead; and his eyelids seemed to be coming out in sympathy with his legs. Rick was the last person to slump to the ground; and as his eyes were blinking closed for the last time he felt sure that he saw a pair of eyes glowing orange and peering in at them through the automatically tinting glass.

-2-

"BOO"! shouted the voice and Rick could feel himself swimming slowly up from the murky depths of his own semi-consciousness. "BOO"! the voice shouted for a second time; and with an awful amount of effort and inner strength Rick opened his eyes and he tried his best to focus upon the strange shapes that were lurking in front of him.

"Now; this would *normally* be the point where I would throw a bucket of water all over you and you would cough and splutter until you were properly awake"! the same voice that had been shouting BOO at him went on to tell him. "But water is a very scarce and precious commodity down here; and so you will have to make do with me shouting BOO"!

"W-w-what"? Rick stuttered.

"BOO"! the person shouted once again.

"Will you *please* stop shouting BOO at me"!

"Aha………..properly awake me thinks"!

"Yoda………is that you; I thought that you died of old age in Return of the Jedi"!

"What"?

"Not seen that one then"?

Rick concentrated really hard and he took a look around. They were certainly within another cave………of that much he was reasonably sure given the rockiness of the walls and the ground and everything. Wooden poles abounded; each of them about an inch lower than the rocky ceiling and running the length of the cave; and to these poles he and the Inspector and the American Agents et al were bound by their wrists; each of them standing on their own two feet but all with their hands hoisted above their heads; all of them in a state of unconsciousness and Dr Foxy the only one dressed in anything more than her undergarments.

Rick looked down; and to his embarrassment he found that he too was wearing only his boxers; and then his embarrassment quickly turned to horror when he discovered that the person who had been shouting BOO at him the whole time was a very attractive looking female who was curvy in all of the right places.

"You seem to have me at a bit of a disadvantage; especially when it comes to the clothes upon my back"! Rick told the sultry temptress with the gravelly voice who had been shouting BOO at him. "Which sort of reminds me………..where *are* the clothes that were once upon my back"?

"We have burnt them all…………..just in case you were wearing listening devices of any kind"! the sultry temptress admitted. "My name is Pearl; I have a steady boyfriend by the name of Will so don't you go getting all Stockholm syndrome on me"!

"Rick" and Rick divulged his name. "And I am very glad that you are happy in your personal affairs. Why are we all trussed up like the last turkeys in the shop at Christmas"?

"We *always* tie up spies and hang them from the ceiling poles"! Pearl was honest. "We don't really come across enough of the spies for this to have become a tradition………you are the first, as it happens; but it was decided some time ago that if we were ever bothered by the spies then we would burn their clothes and hang them from the ceiling poles"!

"But we are not spies"! Rick barked and he was sure that he had awoken Bruno in doing so.

"Well; you *are* going to say that, aren't you; but you didn't let me finish"! Pearl protested. "We *always* tie up spies and hang them from the ceiling poles……………just before we kill them to death"!

"But we are not spies"! Rick once again protested.

"Not spies……….then let us take a look at the evidence"! Pearl suggested. "You were found on a Government train; eating Government crisps and drinking Government stamped whisky"! Pearl summed up with a bit of a sneer. "I am no legal genius but I am thinking that you would be needing one *hell* of a defence council"!

"Look; the train on which we were discovered; where was it bound"? Rick asked of Pearl.

"Up the line…………probably to the City and your swanky pads and your big and fat pensions"! Pearl was sure. "While we live here in squalid underground caves and have to forage for water and enough scraps of food to feed ourselves; *all in this together are we*……….my arse"! and Pearl raised a whippy looking branch from an ash tree with which she was determined to do Rick some damage.

"PUT THAT WHIPPY BRANCH DOWN"! boomed the voice of some authority which belonged to a man dressed in the same orange overalls that Pearl was wearing. "These are no spies; we intercepted a radio signal just after we got them off the train; if they had made it as far as Cardiff then they were to be slaughtered upon the platform as soon as they got off"!

"Well thank goodness for the voice of bloody reason"! Rick sighed. "We would be grateful for a lot of the cutting down………and also for the lending of some clothes as I understand that ours have been burnt; and while we are on the subject of clothing I was wearing rather an ornate looking belt when you people came across us………..I should very much like that belt back"!

"There were indeed *many* belts like that…………in fact I would go so far as to say that there were only three people in your party that did *not* possess such ornate looking belts"! the man with some authority told Rick; and for the time being Rick had forgotten all about the time travelling antics of the American agents. "Now; your clothes have *not* been burnt; I think that was just Pearl getting a bit carried away; and you shall have your belongings back in a very short while; but we need to establish a few of the basics first. What say we just give you your essential clothes back for the time being so that you feel more comfortable and agreeable to us sitting down and having a nice little chat before we do anything else"!

"It would be smashing if you could cut us down a bit as well"? Rick plea bargained.

"But that goes without saying; you can't very well go getting yourselves dressed with your hands tied all the way up there"! and the man with some authority chuckled a friendly little chuckle.

The names of the American agents had all been sewn into the collars and waistbands of their black suits, so matching the suits up to their owners was not proving to be the Herculean task. But it did take a goodly ten minutes of good old fashioned trial and error and the agents trying on pretty well every white shirt of differing sizes before they were all happy and comfortable and able to finish dressing themselves; but each and every agent was thoughtful enough to make some very gracious noises when it came to the laundering and ironing of their clothes.

Rick made sure that he and Bruno only received the *really* ornate looking belts that had *Made in Taiwan* imprinted upon the leatherwear; and as the agents checked over their firearms and their supply of ammunition Rick and Bruno, together with the detectives, the agents and Dr Foxy all sat down at the end of a vast table that veritably filled a communal area of some kind.

"So………….they only went and bloody did it then"? said the man of some authority who introduced himself as Roger.

"Did what…………and who"? the Inspector did wonder before anybody else could get a word in.

"Those bloody Governmental twats"! Roger explained. "Renewable was their latest bloody stupid buzzword; renewable bloody this and renewable bloody that; well…………they *really* cocked things up with their bloody renewable wind turbines, didn't they………..the dickheads; and then it was rumoured that they had found a way to crawl like the maggots they are into a parallel dimension and do everything all over again just to prove that they weren't wrong in the first bloody place; it's all about saving face with that load of bloody tossers"!

"So we have heard"!

"Heard from who………….that bloody Tenby MkII lot; that bloody Tenby MkII lot *are* the bloody Governmental types……what is left of them; and they can't even get their own sewers sorted out. Since you have been underground with us have you *once* smelled a bit of sewer stench or found yourselves up to your ankles in your own piss"?

"Um…………..not as yet"! the Inspector was honest.

"No you bloody haven't; and nor bloody will you"! Roger informed them quite emphatically; and then Roger clapped his hands twice so that attendants who were carrying the large jugs of beer knew to enter the room and start with the filling of their guest's earthenware tankards. "And I bet that the Tenby MkII lot have only told you half a bloody story as well"!

"Um...........to properly know if we have only been told half of a story we would have to be told the *full* story"! Agent Statler was sure.

"And that would be why I have clapped my hands twice and sent for the bloody beer"! Roger explained. "Now; please make sure that you are all bloody sitting comfortably and I shall tell you all about it"!

"Um.............I think that we are all bloody ready"! and as the Inspector spoke for everybody at that bottom end of the table he was aware that some of Roger's personality was rubbing off on him.

"Where to bloody begin is the problem"! Roger was sure. "But to give you the *whole* story then I think that I had better start with our bloody education system……..as was"! Roger decided; and he took a big swig from his earthenware tankard before he began. "You see; we used to have such a wonderful system of education for our bloody children; schools of high quality learning for the academics………and technical schools where a trade could be learnt for the more pragmatic students. This is the best part of forty bloody years ago………but it was then or thereabouts that our Government started with their adoration of the buzzwords………..and *comprehensive* education was their very first buzzword; and after two decades of ever-decreasing standards it became painfully apparent that comprehensive education could never work; and so the Government dumbed down the marking process time and time again to that success for all, another of their bloody buzz-phrases, could be achieved…………and I think it was *then* that the rot really started to kick in. Kids weren't being taught much of anything anymore………let alone a bloody trade. The first thing to go were the engineers; old ones retired and their just weren't any new ones coming up through the ranks because all of our poorly educated and under-achieving kids were in universities doing Mickey Mouse courses in cake-making and modern bloody dance"!

"They seemed to do all right with their wind turbine making"! Dr Foxy pointed out.

"Hah………the making of the turbines was subbed out to contractors in the southern hemisphere; which was also where you had to go if you wanted a bridge built in this bloody country"! and Roger sighed with great emotion as he spoke. "So, more and more of the bloody wind turbines went up because their newest buzzword was the aforementioned *renewables*………and before anybody knew any bloody different all the hot air and sand was blown up from the Tropics and we became a wasteland nation full of sand, cake makers and modern bloody dancers"!

"Thinking about it………with some of the hindsight and everything; I have seen many of the older individuals and also many of the very young; but nothing much in the way of anything in between"! the Inspector realised. "So what has become of all of your recent university leavers and those who would by now be in their thirties"?

"Well............in a move that was very unusual for them our Government of the day admitted that they had been wrong when it came to the whole comprehensive education idea; and they also realised that there were far too many graduates of the Mickey Mouse school of life all becoming a vast drain on society so the Government kicked them all out.........mostly to the southern hemisphere where they were told to go and learn a *real* trade in the countries that we once used to call the Third World"!

"It seems that irony is not without a sense of humour"! Agent Statler presumed quite sadly.

"That is *also* a line from The Matrix"! DC Wiseman was sure.

"Indeed"! and Roger managed to ignore DC Wiseman as he carried on with his story. "And so here we are in a bit of a mess; the sands came and swallowed everything. We have managed to construct a fine system of underground caves, as you can well see; but we can't really do anything that much when it comes to founding a new civilisation when everything up top is a barren wasteland"!

"I can see your predicament"! Agent Statler kindly afforded Roger. "So........how many of there are you down here"?

"Two hundred souls; all doomed to die one by one until there is nobody left...............not even a reminder. It is the children I feel sorriest for; this is all a bit of adventure for them at the moment; little do they know"!

"I actually think that I can foresee a solution to *all* of our problems" Agent Statler said with a smile and a wink and he motioned to one of the jug bearers to have his earthenware tankard topped up.

"We are not having the bloody students back.........we will happily die out first after smothering our youngest in their beds rather than have them back"! Roger was sure.

"That will not be necessary...........your Mickey Mouse students can stay where they are; but the fact remains that we have come here on a mission"! Agent Statler started to explain to Roger. "We are painfully aware that some of your politicians have infiltrated key positions of power in our own dimension;

our plan was obliterate what remains of your Government in *this* dimension and then to destroy the gateway thing when we are safely back on the other side; and we were hoping that with *that* done your politicians already on *our* side would simply give up the ghost because they will have nobody to prove themselves right to; but just in case they don't we need a bit of a backup plan………so how would you feel about uprooting your people and bringing them back with us so that we can continue to root out the evil on the other side………and that much should be fairly easy for you to do what with you knowing all of their faces and everything"!

"That indeed sounds like one heck of a plan"! Roger was sure. "And this offer is definitely open to all two hundred of us…….women and children and everyone"?

"The young children yes; but none of the Mickey Mouse students…………..family members or otherwise; we already have more than enough of those"!

"Then we will gladly help you"!

"You might want to start by putting the wheels back on the train"! Rick suggested.

Chapter Fourteen

"Right then; the problem as I see it is the access"! Agent Statler was sure and he drew maps on the sheets of paper that Roger had provided to illustrate his principle and also to try to explain the lie of the land to Roger. "The problem lies here; this elevator thing is a huge bottleneck; if we can only get down there ten at a time then they could just wait at the bottom and pick us off one by one; and I feel quite sure that these people will have some weaponry that is much more up to date than just the branches of trees………whippy or otherwise"! and Agent Statler anticipated the remark that Bruno was surely about to make.

"I have been down there twice now; and I didn't see anything in the way of weapons……..apart from those ash branches; and I can assure you that they do come bloody tight"! Rick was sure on both accounts.

"Look; if they possess more sophisticated weaponry than that and they wanted to keep it a secret then they surely wouldn't have it out on display"! Agent Statler was sure.

"And *you* are assuming that we would be going in through the front door"! and Roger laughed a laugh that was happy for the most part but also tinged with some insanity.

"Do you mean that there is another way"? and Agent Statler was suddenly all ears.

"Oh yes; it pongs the fair bit mind you..........but I dare say that you will get used to that after a while"!

"Pongs"? Agent Statler wondered for it was not a word that he had heard before.

"It smells a bit"! Rick translated.

"Pongs to high heaven it does........but it makes perfect sense"! Roger was sure. "We can't go overland because it would take too long and I think that the Governmental types are up to something; and I think that those same types will somehow be monitoring the progress of the train so we can't very well use that..........so we will have to use *the pipe*"!

"The pipe"?

"Aye……….*the pipe*"! and Roger pulled aside a curtain and he revealed a huge and metal circular door that was set into the wall. Roger pressed at a few buttons and he turned a wheel in the middle of the door and with a *hiss* the seal was broken and Roger quite easily pulled the huge and metal door open.

"Behold…………*the pipe*"! said Roger and he proudly pointed at the exposed pipe way that was some six feet in diameter and very dark and smelly.

"What the hell is *that* all about"? Agent Statler wondered.

"Well; as previously maintained a few times already this is what we call *the pipe*; back in the day it used to connect a power station that wasn't that far from here to a petro-chemical plant not that far from the old Tenby; *the pipe* here runs straight to Tenby………and then along the coast for a bit"! Roger explained.

"It looks very dark in there"! the Inspector noticed as he peered into the void. "And what will we do……..*walk* to Tenby"?

"Hell no; we have our own little electric choo-choo; and when the time is right we shall switch on the tunnel lights and everything so you will be able to see where you are going…….although you will be inside a pipe so there is only one way to go; it's just that everything has to be battery powered because of the risk of explosion what with there once being oil in there; and at the moment the batteries are all on charge. But rest assured everything will be ready for you to leave first thing in the morning……….which happens to be *really* good timing on your behalf because tonight just happens to be our friendly quiz night"!

"Oh; will the *saints* preserve us"! the Inspector grumbled.

"I know………….I bet you can't believe your luck; all the beer you can drink…………and prizes galore too"!

"What sort of prizes"?

"Well……….free beer mostly; there isn't a right lot of anything else"!

"What the hell is that"? the Inspector wondered the very next morning; and he did some of the pointing as well so that his question would not be misunderstood.

"That is our little choo-choo that I was telling you all about; or the little inspection cart jobbie as it is also known"! Roger said quite proudly and he polished bits and pieces upon the cart with his shirt sleeve as he spoke. "We are pretty sure that it was used for maintenance and inspection purposes when this pipeline was functional; she has a fully enclosed electric motor so there is no danger of it igniting any leftover fumes; it is battery powered and it fairly tears along like Holy shit off a shovel.......but we have manufactured a couple of wagons that can be attached so that a goodly number of passengers can be accommodated and that keeps the speed down to about forty miles an hour. The passenger wagons are already attached and in the pipeline...........we have found it better for the little choo-choo to *push* rather than to *pull*"!

"How long will it take us to get there"? Agent Statler wondered.

"I don't know; how long did it take you to get *here*"?

"That much I cannot remember; you drugged us with something and the whole day is a bit of a fog"! Agent Statler reminded Roger.

"Oh yes; fair point; it'll probably take about three quarters of an hour, give or take; *the pipe* is much quicker than the old road network because it goes in pretty much a straight line"!

"Right then; no time like the present"! the Inspector presumed out loud.

"A dozen of my best men will be accompanying you; to show you what to do when you reach the other end of *the pipe* and you are wanting to get to Tenby MkII"!

"That was to be my very next question"! Agent Statler was honest.

"I spy with my little eye something beginning with P"!

"Pipeline"! the two wagons full of American agents all guessed correctly.

"You lot are too good for me"! Bruno laughed. "Are we nearly there yet; I am fairly bored shitless"!

"Almost there now"! one of Roger's finest men promised him.

"You said the same thing about two hours ago"! Bruno complained.

"To be fair……….I actually said that about two minutes ago which was when you asked the very same question; but honestly, I can assure you that we are very nearly there now. Do you see that red light flashing up there in the distance"? and one of Roger's finest men pointing to the red and flashing light.

"Yes……….I can see it"!

"Well……….that is our stop; we put the red light there on previous excursions so that we didn't overshoot"!

"There seems to be no end in sight to the pipeline though"! the Inspector had noticed.

"No; the pipeline goes on for a goodly few miles after that; all the way past Tenby MkII and onto the refinery; but we don't want to go that far"!

"I hope that I am not smelling a rat"! the Inspector whispered to Agent Statler.

"I don't think so"! Statler whispered back with an air of confidence. "But just in case you are you had better have one of these"! and Statler handed to the Inspector one of his spare 9mm Colt Government Automatics.

"Um……….I do not think that this is a part of Tenby MkII that I have ever seen before"! the Inspector sounded sure and he rested his hand upon the grip of the spare pistol that he had tucked into the waistband of his trousers.

"You *have* actually……….if you came down in the lift, at least; but you have probably not seen it from this angle is all"! said the individual who was one of Roger's finest men who went by the name of Andy. "Allow me to demonstrate"! and Andy drew back a large curtain that had previously been covering a large window. "Now then………tell me what you see before you"?

"Bloody hell; water……………..and lots of it"! the Inspector realised quite incredulously.

"Is this the reservoir thing that we passed at the bottom of the lift shaft"? Rick wondered.

"That it is; although it is an artesian well and not a reservoir………but you have the general gist"!

"So how the hell do we get into Tenby MkII *that* way"? Rick was still curious. "We are beneath the water"!

"Through that door"! and Andy pointed.

"But if we open that door then all the water will surely flood in here and we will all be drowned"! Bruno was sure.

"Well……….that is the outer door to a bit of an airlock affair, actually; we close the outer door, the inner door opens and you swim to the top and to dry land"!

"And I hope that there are all manner of scuba tanks and the like"? the Inspector hoped.

"Not necessary; just come over here and have a look at this"! and as Andy stepped closer to the window as many as they could also stepped closer so that they might see whatever it was Andy was trying to show them; and then Andy asked all of them to look up.

"From this airlock you will only be some ten feet from the surface; it is just a question of holding your various breaths for a few seconds"!

"Holding our breaths"?

"Absolutely; we have done it hundreds of times when on foraging missions"! Andy assured them. "Look; it is my intention to go with you; if you like I will gladly go first so you can see that there is none of the funny business going on"! he volunteered.

"We will go with you"! Rick promised on his and Bruno's behalf. "We shall be first out of the airlock………just in case you encounter any resistance"! which was Rick's way of saying *just so you do not slaughter us with any hidden weaponry as we are swimming to the surface.*

"That sounds like a plan"! Andy was sure. "Shall we……."? and he ushered Rick and Bruno, along with four more of Roger's best men, toward the outer door to the airlock.

"So far.........so good"! Rick whispered as Agent Statler was the last of the American agents to clamber over the bun wall that made up the top of the artesian well. "We will have to pop over to the other side of the reservoir and first disable the guard somehow"!

"Leave that to us"! and Andy had picked up on Rick and Agent Statler's whispering; and Andy selected a few more of Roger's best men for the mission. "We shall give them a taste of the nerve gas that you lot sampled only yesterday"!

"Agent Astoria will accompany you; keep us informed of the goings on"!

"Yes Sir"!

"The rest of us should wait here until the guard are suitably comatose"! the Inspector suggested to Agent Statler and everybody agreed that that was probably the best course of action. "They might only have the ash branches for weapons but they don't half come tight"! Bruno reminded them.

"Um…………guys; are you sure that you have sent us to the right place; there are none of the guards in here"! Agent Astoria shouted only a few minutes after their departure. "We have been all the way through their barracks……..there is not a soul about"!

"Perhaps they have been called to a disturbance in town"? the Inspector wondered.

"That might well be it; there are only half a dozen spare uniforms in there and their supply of whippy ash branches looks to be completely exhausted"! and by now Agent Astoria had walked back along the side of the artesian well and he had rejoined Agent Statler and the others.

"Everybody……….safeties off"! Statler barked to his men in relation to their weapons. "I am not necessarily saying that you should shoot on sight; but I think that we should tread very carefully from now on"!

"Come on then; let's have another look at the town"! and Rick was about to lead the way before Agent Statler called him back.

"You must stay behind the guns from now on"! Agent Statler explained; and Rick had heard enough about the American phenomenon that was friendly fire to take on board just was Statler was saying.

Five minutes later found them standing on the platform that overlooked Tenby MkII; and they found themselves staring down on a deserted town.

Agent Statler despatched two small teams to investigate the homes and the pub just in case the apparently deserted nature of the town was down to a fun quiz or the like; but the teams soon returned having spotted nothing and nobody.

"Shit; they are going to the gateway thing………..and once through it they will destroy it and all of a sudden it is a case of *them* leaving *us* here"! the Inspector realised. "Come on; to the lift; we must get outside and to the top of the nearest sand dune and see if we can see any sign of them; at least they haven't got the bullet train to use and they can't have travelled at night because of the worms"!

Rick and Bruno were the first to make it to the sand dune that overlooked both Tenby MkII in one direction and its railway station in the other; and they just caught sight of the backs of the heads of the Tenby MkII guardsmen as they disappeared into the tunnel that headed in the direction of Cosheston.

"They have just this minute gone into the tunnel"! Rick shouted and he pointed as the others finally caught up with them. "They are on foot so the game is not over yet"!

"We can't follow them into the tunnel………we would be sitting ducks if they have weapons other than the whippy branches of ash which I am suspecting to be the case"! the Inspector was sure.

"That's all right; we shall follow them *above* ground"! Andy was sure.

"But what if the worms attack"? Agent Statler worried for everybody; everybody except Andy it would appear who just smiled at him.

"Oh………….I am counting on the intervention of the worms"!

Chapter Fifteen

"What the bloody hell are you doing"? the Inspector wondered; the alarm all too evident in his trembling voice.

"Just saying hello"! Andy replied; and he was *still* smiling.

Together they had run down the sand dune, across the station's ornate footbridge and up the other side of the dune; and now Andy was leaning over the side of a gaping precipice as he swung a rucksack into the mouth of the northbound railway tunnel.

"We need to bring the mouth of the tunnel down; and there might also be a few nerve agents in that rucksack that might well waft in their direction"! Andy was honest as his bomb went off and the sand beneath all of their feet shook and the mouth of the northbound tunnel came tumbling down. "Now there is no way back for them"!

"Brilliant; but that bomb will surely have attracted the attention of the worms"! Bruno was sure.

"Well if that didn't then this surely will"! and Andy let fly with a few small hand grenades. "For now we should run to that rocky outcrop over there"! and Andy pointed. "The worms cannot traverse over rock and they are always a bit on the grumpy side when they first surface"!

"I am wondering why we didn't leave you back in Port Talbot"! Agent Statler was honest.

"Ah……….but just wait until you see what *we* are going to do"! Andy said; *still* smiling.

-2-

The rocky outcrop wasn't exactly huge when it came to the rocky outcrops in general; so much so that many of the American Agents had to sit upon one another's shoulders and Rick had the pleasure of the foxy Dr Foxy sitting upon his lap.

"Do *not* get any of the funny ideas"! Dr Foxy warned Rick. "You are young and no doubt *full* of the stampeding hormones but this is a seating arrangement borne out of necessity and nothing more"!

"You're the boss"! Rick said without once batting an eyelid; and he flashed a smile at the foxy Dr Foxy which fuelled all of her fears when it came to the youngster and his raging hormones.

"I think that the worms are coming"! Bruno seemed sure; and to reinforce his point he pointed at the ripples in the sand which were growing ever bigger.

"I think that we are quite the sitting ducks up here"! Rick told the rockbound party and the foxy Dr Foxy was at least grateful for the attracting of his attention away from their seating arrangement. "I never once thought that I would spend the end of my days inside of a giant sand worm"!

"Nobody is going to die on account of the worms; well.......nobody in *this* party anyway"! Andy assured everybody. "You should all have a bit of faith. Now; when it comes to the worms you should not let them frighten you or intimidate you in any way........they are mostly all mouth and trousers. You see, they are not really *sand worms*; they are much more used to life on the open sea; only coming ashore to breed and lay their eggs and everything; so if they are disturbed when they are *at it* then they are usually fairly grumpy to begin with"!

"That much can be understood"! Rick was sure.

A pair of sand worms, or ocean-going worms as they were now known to be, burst up from the sand of the desert like sleek and black rockets; their bodies seemingly going on and on in a never ending display of segmented worm bodies; their combined roar as loud as a thousand very angry lions.

"Well now.............we seem to have summoned two of the very old gentlemen; bloody enormous this pair are"! Andy shouted over the worm cacophony. "These two might not be the fastest but they are by far the biggest that we have ever encountered and they are also the most bad tempered.........so watch yourselves and don't do anything that you have not been asked to do"!

"Um…………perhaps we should wait around for some smaller ones…………..as speed is of the essence and everything"? Bruno suggested.

"No…………in hindsight these two are perfect; and we don't really want any of the *really* fast ones when there are so many of the first-timers in the party"! Andy was sure and still smiling. "If we had some of the faster ones then people would surely fall off and we would waste a lot of time circling around to pick them up again"!

"Fall off *what*"? and all of a sudden Bruno was sounding quite terrified.

"The worms of course; we shall ride them as far as the little station just over the dune from the dimension gate"!

"You are surely having a laugh"! Bruno was sure.

"This really *is Dune* with Kyle MacLachlan"! Rick was also sure; but Andy just pulled a funny face. "You haven't seen that one then"?

"The worms are not to be feared"! Andy was adamant.

"So if the worms are not to be feared then why are we now all sitting on top of one another on top of this bloody rock"? Dr Foxy wondered.

"Because when the worms first break surface they are really quite annoyed and as bad tempered as hell………as has already been established; but as soon as they realise it is us they calm down very quickly"!

"Okay…………assuming that you are not winding us up and we are actually supposed to ride on top of these worms, then how the bloody hell do we get up there"? Rick wondered. "Those things are absolutely bloody enormous"!

"I am *so* glad that you asked me that; what is about to come up next is the *really* clever bit"!

After a few minutes of the worms crashing around the desert like the most bad tempered creations in existence; and after a few more minutes of the soothing talk on behalf of Andy and his men, the worms soon calmed down as had been promised; and they stopped with their cavorting and they lay down side by side beside the nearest sand dune.

"So what do we do now……..run to the top of the dune and jump off"? Bruno was heard to wonder.

"Now you are just being daft; no………the pilots will go up first; and just as soon as they are ready they will drop down the ropes and then we can all climb up and sit down on top"! Andy explained.

"Pilots………….you have *worm pilots*"?

"Well yes; the worms would have to be steered otherwise they'd end up going all over the bloody shop"!

"It would have to be a bloody big bridle to fit around a head the size of *that*"! and Bruno pointed.

"Well………….I can see the way that you are thinking but it doesn't quite work like that; you see…….the worms have a ring of blowholes that go all the way round them just behind their heads………very similar to those of whales but a lot more of them; all you have to do is watch………….Pilot Emlyn is just about to get mounted up"! and Andy pointed out the thickset man whose arms were full of ropes.

Pilot Emlyn approached the nearest of the great beasts; all the time making soothing *who's a good boy* noises. Pilot Emlyn located one of the blowholes and he stuck a great big metal hook into it which made the worm grunt the fair bit; and the rope that was attached to the end of the great big and metal hook he coiled around his right arm.

Done with its grunting the huge worm started slowly to roll over; taking the hook *and* Pilot Emlyn up into the air. When Pilot Emlyn was in a position that was roughly perpendicular the giant worm stopped with its rolling and Pilot Emlyn waved to those upon the ground before he disappeared from sight.

"I am guessing that he wasn't supposed to fall off the other side"? Bruno presumed.

"In a perfect world, no; but then Pilot Emlyn hasn't been at being a pilot for very long"! Andy explained. "Pilot Caravan……….please show your brother how it is supposed to be done"!

Pilot Caravan, who looked to be the younger of the two brothers, mounted the same beast as his brother had chosen and in exactly the same manner as his brother had done. But when the worm stopped turning and Pilot Caravan was perpendicular he inserted a second big and metal hook into a second blowhole; and the rope from this second hook he wrapped around his *left* arm and he held onto the ropes like they were reins upon a giant horse before he kicked a third rope over the side of the beast.

"Another of our men will now climb up using that rope; and he in turn will drop down another rope and so on until everybody is aboard"! Andy explained.

"And the worms will definitely not attempt to go back underground"! Bruno worried.

"Not with us riding upon their backs; the worms are our friends. Oh………and you will be needing these as well"! and Andy handed over two pairs of goggles that looked as though they had been purloined from a swimming pool.

After only another two or three minutes the worms were both fully loaded up with their human cargo and Pilot Caravan shouted for the worms to get along; which they did; and very quickly too.

"Jesus Christ…………..if these are the slow ones then I would probably hate hitching a lift on a GTi version"! Rick shouted above the deafening roar of the wind as the enormous beasts fairly rocketed along.

"Magnificent, aren't they; and they can keep up this pace all day"! Andy shouted back with some pride. "We have already overtaken those within the tunnel; a few more minutes and we will be sitting by the dimension jumping gate waiting to unleash one unholy surprise………..and that horrible lot will not know one single thing about just what is hitting them"!

Pilot Caravan steered his worm over the top of the dune and they started down the sandy hill toward the small and rural station that they all knew so well.

"Take us up to the dune that is just over there"! the Inspector shouted to Pilot Caravan and he pointed out the dune that he was referring to. "If we were to just sit down and wait for them to come out of the tunnel then we run the risk of them being able to get themselves dug in and give us a bit of a fight; but if we hide behind the dune that is overlooking Cosheston and the dimension gate thing and we wait until the last minute before we attack then they will have nowhere to hide; they will be stuck in open desert"!

"Good thinking"! Agent Statler agreed with the Inspector. "We can just keep our heads down behind that ridge and when they start climbing the dune my men can cut them to pieces with machine gun fire; and there will be nothing at all friendly about that"!

Pilot Caravan made his turn long and slow so that they would not be betrayed by any worm marks in the sand; and as they approached the top of the sand dune the worm that was *not* being piloted by Pilot Caravan was transformed into an exploding mass of worm-goo and dead agents as it was hit by single and cataclysmic shot from a huge weapon of some kind.

"Holy shit……….the rumours were correct; they *have* developed a bloody laser cannon and I think that it is *us* that have been drawn into a bloody trap"! screeched Pilot Caravan and he leapt from the head of the worm; and after a neat forward roll he was running across the sand roughly in the direction of Port Talbot as fast as his legs would carry him.

The surviving members of Roger's best men were not that far behind him.

"Right…………everybody off the worm and get back down the dune to the small and rural station"! Agent Statler screamed; and they all slid down the side of the worm and started with their sprinting toward the small rural stop.

They heard the blast and then the subsequent thumping to the ground of various worm bits as their own poor worm was blasted into smithereens; and one by one the slower moving agents at the rear of the fleeing party were picked off with more of the deadly laser fire.

"I just *knew* that they must have weapons other than the ash branches…………no matter *how* whippy they are"! the Inspector said aloud as they assembled in the small ticket office come waiting room.

"If it is a fight to the death that they want then a fight to the death they will God damn have"! Agent Statler announced as he dug various concealed pistols out of his socks and underpants and the like. "Only *I* shall not be dying on this day……….I will tell you *that* much for nothing"! he was sure; a matter of mere seconds before a shot from a laser gun of some description blasted his head from his shoulders and neatly cauterised the wound before his lifeless and headless body even fell to the ground.

More laser blasts started to hit them from their right flank now as what was obviously the second party of Tenby MkII troops started to emerge from the railway tunnel; but the keen eyes of the remaining American Agents soon cut the second party down to nothing as they found themselves pinned down in the mouth of the tunnel.

"Talk about an ambush and *then* some"! said Agent Astoria. "I never even saw it coming"!

"Grenade…………take cover"! shouted a surviving American Agent; and then the lights went out.

Chapter Sixteen

In the chaos that ensued following one of the surviving American Agents accidentally shooting the light fitting from the ceiling Agent Astoria, in a moment of extreme self-sacrifice and generosity, had thrown himself on top of the grenade device that had been fired or lobbed into the small ticket office come waiting room affair at the rural station. But then so had Agents Moulder and Scully, the only other surviving American Agents.

To all outward appearances the grenade device had seemed rather on the small side; but it delivered one hell of a punch and the American Agents were all blown into very small pieces.

Rick and Bruno, the detectives and the foxy Dr Foxy were the only living survivors within the crumbling remains of the ticket office come waiting room; and the power of the blast was such that it had rendered them rather disorientated and very deaf.

"You will come with us"! said the man in the uniform of blue who also sported a rifle that looked like something fresh out of a science fiction film; and he pointed said rifle at them.

"I didn't catch a *word* of that"! the Inspector said very loudly. "I have tinnitus in my ears like a bell ringer's practise in a sodding cathedral"!

"You will get up and come with us"! the man with the laser blasting rifle reiterated; but louder this time.

"Chicken soup"? screeched Dr Foxy.

"No……..he was asking about our tetanus jabs"! Bruno was sure.

"Oh…………for the love of *God*"! the man in the uniform of blue and the laser blasting rifle cursed and he walked over to the notice board that was mounted to the only wall still standing in the once proud ticket office come waiting room and he started to write upon the wipe-clean part of the board.

Get up and come with us; there is somebody who would speak with you the man wrote. *And none of the funny stuff!*

"My balance has all gone to shit"! Bruno noticed very loudly as he was the first of them to stagger to his feet. "It is quite like being pissed but with none of the expense"!

"That will be the blast from the grenade thing messing with your ears"! the Inspector shouted.

"I actually heard some of that; and *you* must have heard *me*; our ears must be getting better"! Bruno was sure.

They were marched out of the remains of the ticket office come waiting room and across the battle scarred platform; and all the time many laser blasting rifles were pointed at them as they were escorted to the top of the nearest dune.

When they reached the top of the dune and they were able to look down the other side they could see the kitchen at number thirteen as clear as day; and they were marched down the dune and toward the kitchen and also toward a group of laser rifled soldiers who were all sitting cross legged in the sand as a man stood upon a box and addressed them.

The man who was standing upon the box and doing all of the talking had his back to them as they approached; but there was something familiar sounding about his voice that they all found vaguely familiar; and when they approached their guard coughed to announce his presence and the man upon the box turned around and he had a good sneer at them.

"Bloody hell.............it's Cookie"! Rick noticed almost straight away.

"What the bloody hell are you doing"? the Inspector wondered. "These are not your people; this is not your fight or even your *dimension*..............you are from *our* world"!

"Ah...........but these *are* my people, as it happens; well........all the ones who prove useful to me anyway"! Cookie replied; his face contorted with sneering and contempt. "There might well be a painter and decorator in *your* dimension that looks just like me..............but in *this* dimension I am Prime Minister Cookson"!

"But The Bluns told us all about you; about your struggle with the tequila and the subsequent break-up of your marriage"! and Bruno was quite sure that he hadn't dreamt all of it up.

"Ah……………The Bluns, you say; perhaps you mean *General* Blunsden……………leader of my crack assassination squad and Deputy Prime Minister to boot"!

"Deputy Prime Minister"?

"Yes………I know; but it was one of those crappy hung parliament affairs; he is indeed pretty shite when it comes to the politics………..but he is great with the troops and he can't half tell a convincing story"! and Prime Minister Cookson's sneer turned into quite a belly laugh. "Tequila slammers my arse"! he chortled.

"And you lot fell for it hook, line and sinker"! said General Blunsden as he appeared upon the sandy scene. The General looked resplendent in his dark blue military uniform that came with a chest full of medals, some lovely gold piping and a laser blasting pistol upon each hip.

"You see; you all arrived on the scene just a little bit too early…………..and I blame those meddling Krauts for that"! Prime Minister Cookson started to explain. "We needed just a few more days for our team in *your* dimension to get themselves fully prepared………..and so we had to continue to find ways to stall you; but we are very grateful to you for sniffing out those rebels in the open desert of Port Talbot………talk about bloody flies in the ointment. I suppose that we could have simply left them for dead when we closed the dimension gate………but it was *so* nice to kill them all first; they have caused us nothing but trouble over the last few months"!

"You are the complete nutjob"! the Inspector told him.

"You say the nicest things"! and the Prime Minister was back to sneering. "Normally flattery like that will get you *everywhere*; but I am afraid that now you will have to die. You see……..I have been fairly agonising over what to do with you; should I kill you…………..or should I just leave you here in the desert to watch as the kitchen to number thirteen suddenly blinks out of existence; but then I worry because I know that you have made friends with the worms and you might survive for long enough to figure out how we came up with the idea for the dimension gate in the first place. So I have decided to err on the side of caution and not take any of the chances……..so it's death for you lot; nothing nasty or sadistic………..just a firing squad.

Just over there you will notice a number of poles sticking up out of the sand…………and if you wouldn't mind moving along a bit in the direction of said poles then we shall tie you to them and provide you with blindfolds and everything and it will all be over in a flash"!

"Look over there; sand worms………thousands of them"! and the Inspector pointed at nothing much more than an empty sand dune; but in the ensuing chaos he managed to draw the pistol that was still secreted within the waistband to his trousers and he shot General Blunsden right between his eyes; which was not particularly outstanding marksmanship on the Inspector's behalf because he had been aiming at Prime Minister Cookson who had been standing a goodly ten paces to the left of the General.

The Colt automatic was smashed from the Inspector's grip and he was wrestled to the sandy ground by two of the Prime Minister's private guards.

"Ah well…………he was a good General; but I never really wanted a deputy Prime Minister in the first place; so……..problem solved"! and Prime Minister Cookson was back to laughing once again. "The electorate of old would probably thank you for that"!

The Inspector was the last of the party to be hoisted to his feet and tied to the only remaining pole that was sticking out of the sand; and a blindfold was dropped over his eyes and tied securely behind his head just like all the others.

"What about the last requests and everything"? Rick wondered.

"Look…………..if there was the time then I would surely indulge you"! Prime Minister Cookson told them in all honesty. "But as time is fairly pressing then I am afraid that there is nothing more to come for you………..except for the shooting; bring on the executioners"!

The five members of the Prime Minister's private guard lined themselves up in front of their five targets; and the guardsmen pressed at the little buttons on their laser blaster rifles that then started to whine as the component parts of their weapons wound themselves up to a crescendo of optimum power so that even with the *poorest* of shooting any shot even *remotely* on target should prove fatal.

"Seeing what you have become used to as far as *food* is concerned in this dimension I realise that a steak dinner might be somewhat hard to come by.........but could we not even have one last cigarette"? Rick continued to wonder as he still harped on about their last requests, or the lack of them.

"Smoking was banned in our super-civilised society many years ago; too harmful to one's health"!

"Probably not as harmful as blowing huge deserts and hot air all around the globe with your bloody wind turbines"! Bruno told the Prime Minister.

"I will freely admit that we might have made a slight miscalculation when it came to the wind turbines of old; but we have learnt from our mistakes and we are about to demonstrate as much in the next dimension over. Firing squad.........get ready"!

"Last E-cigarette then"? Rick tried.

"Take aim"!

There followed an agonising silence of goodness knows how long and all those currently tied to poles all held their breath as they awaited the inevitable; but the agonising silence was broken by a sudden and violent *whooshing* noise from above; followed by a series of small explosions and a lot of confused shouting; and the next thing that anybody who had previously been tied to wooden poles knew was the sensation of being gently lifted from the ground and carried through the air before being put down a short distance away.

"Stay here for now while we finish them off"! they were told.

Rick managed to get his hands free; and he removed his blindfold before helping his friends free of their own bonds. They all looked up in wonderment as to what could be causing the strange whooshing noises from above……..and they were all stunned into silence at what they saw; even though seeing was supposed to be believing.

"Are those people flying about on broomsticks up there"? Bruno wondered with a very slack jaw as he pointed.

"That they are; and the one with all the blue fire erupting from her fingertips looks to be Granny Wrinkles"! the Inspector was sure. "They are the witches from Westhaven; and they really *are* witches; I thought that all they were interested in was a little nookie underneath the stars"!

"In February…………….in Wales; you *have* to be kidding"!

They all spun around to where the voice originated and they found themselves face to face with the warlock Manbooba; and they also found that they were standing just outside the back door to the kitchen at number thirteen.

"We have known of this place and their kind for quite some time now; we knew that they were not wife-swappers but we could not have told you that because you would not have believed us"! Manbooba admitted. "Can I just say that we would never have willingly let them across the threshold into *our* world without a bloody good fight; but as time went on it was soon becoming dangerously apparent that we were growing increasingly outnumbered……..both by the ones yet to come through the gate but also by the ones already here; we tried to match the ones already here in their positions of power but there are simply too many of them"!

"And the blue fire coming from their fingertips"?

"We are witches and warlocks; this is what we do"! and as Manbooba was speaking the entire population of Tenby MkII were blown to bits and the bloodied and semi-conscious Prime Minister Cookson was dropped at his feet.

"Rick.........go and grab one of those laser guns from a dead guardsman"! and the Inspector pointed at the mound of bodies.

"Do not worry about guns; we do not need them"! Manbooba said with a smile; and he blinked once and the wrists and ankles of the prostrate Prime Minister instantly shimmered with glowing ropes of electric blue that prevented him from moving even ever so slightly.

"We cannot take this abomination back to our dimension to stand trial; for starters nobody would believe us when we started on about parallel dimensions..........and those of his people who already hold positions of power might even be able to get him off"! Manbooba explained. "And if we leave him here then he might find a way of reopening the gateway if he was given enough time"!

"There is no other option"! the Inspector agreed.

"Granny will take him away and drop him from a great height onto some rocks or something"! Manbooba volunteered. "There is no need for anyone of us to watch his demise"!

"We need to be sure"! the Inspector was sure.

"You are right, of course; okay…………what about dropping him from a great height onto some rocks when he is on fire with some of that blue shit that the wife does; that should do the trick"!

"Agreed"!

"Hello again Inspector"! said Granny Wrinkles as he broomstick dropped majestically to the ground and she alighted from it. "That is the last of them………apart from *that* evil bastard"! and she pointed at the Prime Minister.

"We have already decided on his fate"! Manbooba told his other half.

"I hope it involves some of the fiery blue shit"!

"That it does, my sweet"!

"What about those already in positions of power in our own dimension"? Granny Wrinkles worried.

"Leave them to us"! Rick told her. "I have a bit of a plan".

-2-

Rick and Bruno stood on the upper floor of the multi-storey car park and they watched as their local Council Headquarters burnt to the ground.

"That's forty of them gone in one fell swoop"! Rick said with a smile. "No more wind turbines down *here* for a while"!

"Two hundred to go then"! and Bruno did the maths.

"It shouldn't take too long"! Dr Foxy was sure as her broomstick dropped majestically from the night sky and she too stood upon the upper floor of the car park and they all admired their own handiwork.

"How about Rick, Bruno and Foxy..........Divine Warriors"? Bruno suggested for they were still trying their hardest to think of a name for their new and privately funded operation.

"I am none too keen on the *divine* bit"! Rick was honest.

"Do you think that this is what Agent Statler meant; you know............when we were in America and he told us that we would be doing something of vital importance with our newly found colossal wealth"? Bruno wondered.

"I am almost certain"! Rick was honest again.

"So...........where to now"? the former Dr Foxy wondered.

"1966.............we need to swap a couple of babies"!

"Like who"?

"David Cameron for John Cusack"!

"The films will be awful"!

THE END

Printed in Great Britain
by Amazon